FROST

a novel by

Douglas Meredith Ready

FROST

Cover designed by Douglas Meredith Ready ©2017

ISBN-13: 978-1546750222

ISBN-10: 1546750223

Published by **DMR Creative Enterprises.**

Printed and Distributed by **CreateSpace, a division of Amazon.**

www.douglasready.com

FROST

To Mona, the love of my life.

FROST

FROST

Chapter One

The look on her face said *I'm pissed and you're handy.*

"Are you Frost." It wasn't a question.

"You can call me Micah." I flashed my sincerest smile, hoping the sparkle in my eyes would soften her a bit. It didn't. She glared at me with all the warmth usually reserved for the morning catbox deposit. "Won't you come in?"

She slapped a manila envelope against my chest. "You want to explain this?"

"Can I get you some coffee?"

"I'm half-an-inch away from suing your ass off, buster. Don't get cute with me."

"I'm always cute. It's a genetic condition." I slid my finger under the glued flap of the envelope and tore it open. I turned and walked to the rocker, dropped into the seat. "You don't have to take the coffee, but do come inside and shut the door."

The woman stomped across the living room and dropped onto the loveseat. She laid a lambskin briefcase on her legs, and kept a double-handed death grip on its handle.

I turned the manila envelope on its side and dumped the contents into my lap. Four photographs—five-by-seven glossies, full color, and professional quality—caught the sunlight. The sun's glare washed away specific detail, but the general impression remained clear.

"You're very pretty when you're naked."

"I ought to kill you, you bastard."

FROST

I tugged at my right earlobe, stretched, pushing my hands against the small of my back. I pushed two fingers into the suede sock clipped inside the waistband of my jeans and palmed the little .25 automatic I kept there. I brought the pistol around in front of me and pointed the ugly little thing at my guest. "What's your name, ma'am?"

"You goddam – "

I cocked the pistol. "Your name?"

"Camey Horne."

"Miss Horne, I'm going to have to ask you to set that briefcase on the floor. Slowly, don't do anything too sudden. That's right. Now, shove it over to me with your foot." I leaned over and pulled the briefcase to me. "Please put your hands in your lap. Palms up." I picked up the photographs and laid them on top of the briefcase.

"So what now? Are you going to shoot me?"

I straightened my legs in front of me and crossed one cowboy boot over the other. "Lady, you got one hell of a lot of nerve."

"*Me???*"

"Yes, you. You show up at my home unannounced, charge in here, threaten to sue me, swear at me, throw dirty pictures in my face, then threaten to kill me. Hell, Miss Horne, I don't even know who you are."

Camey Horne sat for a moment, started to speak once or twice, changed her mind. Autumn sunshine seeped into the room and wrapped a halo around her dark auburn hair. She sighed, her shoulders slumped, and part of the anger seemed to leave her eyes. I relaxed my grip on the gun and laid it against my thigh.

"I don't know if I believe you," she said, finally.

FROST

"Let's promise not to try and kill one another for a few minutes and see if we can figure out what's going on here. Is that okay with you?"

She shrugged. "You're the one with the gun."

I uncocked the pistol and tucked it back inside its holster. "Yeah, and you're the one with a problem." I pushed out of the rocker. "What do you take in your coffee?"

"Black."

"Lady after my own heart." I waltzed Camey down the hall and into the kitchen, poured two mugs of strong, black coffee and set the mugs on the table. I slid into the wooden chair across from her. "Tell me about the pictures."

"They were delivered to my office this morning by courier."

"And you thought I sent them. Why?"

"An email from you with the message *We need to talk* came in about ten minutes after the pictures were delivered."

"I'm unlisted. How'd you find me?"

"Your address was in the email."

"But no phone number?"

"No."

"The man in the pictures, I assume he's married?"

Camey shook her head. "No, he isn't."

"Are you sure?"

"I'm sure."

"Are you? Married, I mean?"

"No."

"Any reason you can think of that the two of you shouldn't be seen together?"

"We live together."

FROST

I sipped the coffee. "Offhand, I'd say somebody wants you to know how easy it is to get to you."

"Not you, though?"

I shook my head. "Not me. Believe me, Camey—may I call you Camey?—if I had a reason to come after you, I'd just show up in person. Dirty pictures are a little bit subtle for me."

"Then why—"

"I don't know." I climbed out of the chair and refilled the coffee mugs. "What's your boyfriend's name?"

"Pearson Stone."

"Why isn't he here?"

Camey drummed her fingers on the table. "He doesn't know about the pictures."

"Why not?"

"They were delivered to me. I got really angry when I saw them. He was out of the office and I didn't want to wait."

"So you work together as well."

"Yes."

"And you decided to come by yourself."

"Yes."

"That wasn't very bright. I could have been dangerous."

Camey pursed her lips. "I was prepared for that."

"If you'd really been prepared the gun would have been in your coat pocket instead of in the briefcase."

Camey turned a dark red. She coughed.

"Where do you work?"

"Pacific Investment, Columbia Tower."

I glanced at my watch. "If you hurry you'll make it back in time for lunch. I'll meet you and Stone at two-thirty in your office."

FROST

"I understand you're some kind of Private Investigator."

"Something like that."

"I have no intention of hiring you, Mr. Frost."

"You can't afford me, Ms. Horne."

Camey Horne glared at me for a moment and then pushed away from the table, stood up and walked back into the living room. "Two-thirty, then. Pear and I will expect you." She picked up her briefcase, knocked the photographs to the floor. "I don't need those. Perhaps they will be of some use to you."

"Perhaps."

The woman opened the front door and walked out. I retrieved the pictures.

The sun shining on them washed out the details when I'd glanced at them earlier. I tilted the first to block the glare. Camey Horne was a lovely woman, but much of her beauty was hidden in the unposed stills. Her face twisted into an assumed ecstasy, but agony was an easy second option.

I knew the man in the photographs. He'd grown a beard since I'd last seen him and he'd put on about a hundred pounds, but there are some people you just don't forget no matter how hard you try.

Camey Horne's boyfriend was my fraternal twin brother.

FROST

Chapter Two

I didn't much look like a lawyer. I'd lost the jeans, replaced them with grey wool slacks, a white button-down collar oxford shirt, burgundy tie and a blue camelhair sport coat, and I'd changed the cowboy boots for a pair of sleek Bally wingtips polished so brightly you could almost see the future in them. The lawyers all wore olive double-breasted suits and brown Italian loafers.

I climbed off of the elevator on the seventeenth floor and found myself in the lobby of Pacific Investment, LTD. The place reminded me of a high-class brothel. Blood red carpet stretched across the length of the room and up a four foot section of wall. Mahogany trim topped the edge of the covered wall and the remainder boasted a rich pearl grey. A series of Steve Hanks' prints, signed and numbered, hung at even interval across the front wall.

I unwrapped a piece of Dentyne and dropped the paper into a gleaming brass spittoon.

"I'm here to see Ms. Horne and Mr. Stone."

"Your name, sir?"

"Micah Frost."

The woman behind the counter—no, the girl, she couldn't have been more than nineteen—picked up the phone on her desk, punched a button on the console and murmured something into the receiver. She stood up and smiled, and I followed her down a short corridor.

FROST

Camey Horne opened the door, a massive mahogany barricade. I stepped inside and Camey told the girl we were not to be disturbed.

Pear walked toward me, his right hand extended. Casually, I tucked both of my hands into my trouser pockets.

"Micah, you never change."

Pear was enormous. He must've weighed three hundred pounds, but he belayed any suggestion of fat. His hairline receded slightly, but a thick growth of neatly trimmed beard knocked away the starkness of all that pink flesh.

Pear moved with a surprising grace. His foot slammed into my crotch, his mammoth fist backhanded me. I fell against the door and slid to the carpet. The gentle office lighting softened even more, first to grey, then to black.

***

Steel bands pinned my arms to my side. I bit my lip and prayed the Tilt-A-Whirl would end its run.

The spinning slowed and I opened my eyes.

Pearson pretended to juggle, bounced my little .25 from one palm to the other. I tried to follow the gun's path, but rolling my eyes brought me one step closer to puking all over my camelhair jacket. I could do without the dry cleaning bill.

I tried to move and couldn't. I glanced down and found my jacket buttoned, the shoulders pulled over the top of the chair I sat in. Simple and too effective.

"Ah", Pear said. "It appears our guest is back among the living."

"You're ruining my jacket."

FROST

Pear strolled around behind me, shoved his hand under the collar of my coat and popped it up over the chair back. The numbness in my arms traded for thousands of steel pins jammed into flesh as the blood began circulating once again."

The big man dropped the .25 into my lap. "If you don't mind, I'd kind of like to keep the bullets." He reached into his trouser pocket and retrieved a handful of small slugs. "As a souvenir."

"Of what?"

"The day I ruined my brother's chances of becoming a parent."

My genitals melded into a great dull throb.

"How long has it been, Micah?"

"Not long enough."

Camey Horne perched on the window sill behind the desk. Her skirt slithered halfway up an excruciatingly beautiful thigh and I wondered what might possess such an incredible beauty to engage in those activities so clearly recorded by Pentax with a three-hundred pound Bozo like Pear.

It couldn't be charm. To the best of my recollection, Pear had none.

I took a long look at my brother. He grinned at me through thickly bearded cheeks. Dom Deluise flashed through my mind, his personality replaced with that of an on-screen insane Jack Nicholson.

I shook my head, hard.

Pear's suit was classic banker, three piece, grey pinstripe. The coat folded back against his arm, hand jammed into his trouser pocket. A Nordstrom label glared at me from beneath the

FROST

inside breast pocket. A Nordie labeled suit tailored to wrap around Pear's bulk would go for two grand, easy.

A Rolex Oyster Perpetual draped across his left wrist, not the top of the line, but certainly not a Timex. If it was a copy it was a damned good one, but something told me the watch was genuine.

He wore black cowboy boots with the Nordie threads. Pear and I shared one physical characteristic, other than parentage, and that was an odd shoe size, size eleven, B-width, long and narrow. Those boots screamed custom-made and that was expensive.

Camey wore a much pricier diamond encrusted Rolex. I don't know a lot about women's clothing, but quality material and a tailored fit are easy to recognize. So is high carat jewelry and Camey decorated her marvelous form with earrings, a bracelet and a couple of rings that probably cost more than my car.

"Tell me, fatboy, how long have you been in Seattle?"

"Three months. How long have you been stalking me?"

"Why would I stalk you?"

"I don't know. Misplaced sense of family unity? Maybe just the desire to be a general nuisance?"

"The term stalking implies I at least have at least a minimal interest in you. I don't. And I've always tried to be a specific nuisance."

"Then why are you here?"

"I came to find out who spoofed my email."

"Camey tells me you've taken up photography." Pear reached into the inside pocket of his suit jacket and produced a flat gold case, opened it and removed a thin, black cigar. "Don't fuck with me, Micah. I have neither the time nor the patience. And don't think that just because you're my brother—"

FROST

"Careful, now, you don't want to get bloodstains all over this fancy carpet."

"It won't show. That's why I picked this color."

Camey sighed. "Are you two going to bicker all day?"

"Tell me, Micah, why would somebody send us dirty pictures from your email address?"

"I'm not much interested in why, I just want to know who to punch for spoofing my account."

"Maybe someone knows you're brothers," Camey offered.

Pear snorted. "It's not come up in any conversation I've had in the last twenty years. Who've you pissed off lately, Micah?"

"Most everybody I've had occasion to deal with." I turned toward Camey Horne. "How long have you known?"

"Pear told me," she said, "after I told him I'd met you."

"What is it you do here, anyway?"

"None of your fucking business."

"I don't liked to be tied to you, Pear."

Pear plopped his butt on the edge of the desk. I'd swear I heard the thing groan. "Let me guess," he said, "you're going to find out who's got the rope?"

"Something like that."

"And since we're family you'll only charge me a nominal fee for cleaning up a mess I'm convinced you created in the first place."

I stood up and slipped the .25 back into its holster.

"You're full of shit, Micah," Pear said.

The spinning eased, the nausea subsided. My groin still ached, but the pain settled into a dull, constant thud I thought I could manage. I shifted my weight from one foot to the other. Pear stood up, stepped in front of me.

FROST

"I take it you can walk?"

"I can walk."

"Then get the hell out of my office."

I slammed my right knee into Pear's crotch, simultaneously slapped an open palm against each of his ears. He doubled over and I spun, drove an elbow into his nose. Blood spurted onto the carpet and the leg of my trousers.

"I'll be damned," I said. "Blood doesn't show on this carpet."

Pear slumped to the floor, both hands crammed between his legs. I picked up his smoldering cigar and shoved it into the gaping inside breast pocket of his suit coat. "Grey isn't your color, Pear. Best to stick with navy blue, maybe black. More slimming."

Camey hadn't moved from the window sill. "I think you'd better go," she said. She climbed down from her perch, not carefully, and her blue knit skirt slid even further up her thighs. She stood, watched me look at her. The tight skirt hovered above lacy, old-fashioned garter clips. "Goodbye, Mr. Frost."

"Miss Horne." I turned and walked out the door, closed it behind me.

The receptionist popped her gum and smiled as I walked past her desk. "Have a nice day," she said.

FROST

Chapter Three

"You're a mess."

"I missed you, too."

"And your hair is getting very long." Chelsea smiled across the table, placed her hand on top of mine. "I like it."

Her blonde hair fell nonchalantly over her left eye. I sighed and silently cursed whatever deity had given her a husband long before I met her. "How's Charles?"

"Still there. Probably always will be unless you'd like to sweep me off my feet and carry me away on your white horse."

"Horse is in the shop. Some kind of transmission problem."

"Just my luck. Could I interest you in a cheap, yet torrid afternoon interlude?"

I quit smoking eleven years ago and would suddenly cheerfully maim for a cigarette. "Somebody ought to paddle your butt."

"I know people who'd pay money to do that."

"How is Kelly?"

"She's madly in love with you, you know. Any day now she'll throw herself at you and then you won't want me anymore."

"I won't want you any less."

"Promises, promises."

I met Chelsea Holmes three years ago. Her daughter Kelly had vanished, and after a week without a ransom note the cops wrote the girl off as just another twelve-year-old runaway. Their

FROST

assessment was correct. Sometimes, though, things on the road don't turn out the way things were planned.

It took me three days to find Kelly. I reached the girl just in time to short-circuit a forced career as a porn actress.

Chelsea and I fell together like an old pair of Levi's and well-worn cowboy boots. It took an entire lifetime to stumble across what should have been the perfect mate, a woman with similar intellect, the same sort of curiosity about the world, the same unwillingness to function in a traditional manner, and an intoxicating sexual magnetism.

I liked Chelsea's husband Charles. I wished that I didn't like Charles, but I did.

I looked into Chelsea's clear blue eyes and reluctantly pulled myself back into reality. "I need a favor, sweetheart."

"*Sweetheart*--when you say that you're supposed to curl your lip and speak with a slight lisp."

"Ever heard of an outfit called Pacific Investment?"

"Over in the tower?"

"Yes."

"What do you know about them?"

"They pay my bill on time."

"Your bill?"

"They're a client. The receptionist is one of my temps."

"Miss Parton works for you?"

Chelsea laughed aloud. "You are a perceptive devil. Yes, Dolly is one of mine. Why do you ask?"

"Have you met Pearson Stone?"

"Indeed. He's quite the charmer. Have you seen the inside of his office?"

"Yeah. Looks like a house of ill repute."

Chelsea shrugged. "Business by definition."

"What do you know about Stone?"

"He dresses well. Wears too much expensive cologne." She frowned. "He strikes me as somebody who could steal your socks without taking your shoes off."

"Ummm."

"How are you mixed up with Pearson?"

"First name basis?"

"Oh, Micah. You know how we floozies are."

I gave Chelsea a thumbnail sketch of what happened, pointedly leaving out the fisticuffs and the fact that Pear was my long-lost sibling.

"Do you still have the pictures?"

"Why do you ask?"

"If you're making copies..."

"Chelsea! I'm shocked!"

"I've never seen a three-hundred pound man naked."

"What do you know about the company?"

"I love your company."

"Pacific Investments."

"Oh. I can get you a copy of my file. Annual reports, promo stuff, things like that. Would that help?"

"Couldn't hurt."

"I'll messenger it to you before I leave the office," she said, then grinned. "Or I could bring it myself."

"No, you couldn't."

"Now you've done it," Chelsea said evenly. "You've gone and hurt my feelings."

***

FROST

I turned off the hot water bit by bit, allowed the cold stream to pound against my shoulders and then cupped my hands around my testicles to allow a semi-soak in what I hoped would be a healing bath.

It wasn't.

I lightly toweled off, wrapped the frayed bath cloth around my waist and retrieved my clothing from the bathroom floor. The blazer would go to the drycleaners, the white shirt would drop into the hamper for washing. I tossed the into the garbage pail. My usual mode of dress is jeans, boots and a sweater, with a sport coat if the occasion calls for spiffiness. I own two suits, a Brooks Brothers blue and a Ralph Lauren grey pinstripe, and two pairs of Nordstrom worsted wool dress slacks, one grey and one black. I bought the entire wardrobe on the same day for less than a hundred dollars at Value Village. I've worn each suit twice, the dress slacks maybe half-a-dozen times. I didn't think I'd miss the grey slacks. Anyway, it didn't make much sense to spend fourteen bucks to dry clean a pair of nine dollar britches.

I pulled on a red cotton polo shirt and a pair of black faded jeans, opted for a pair of old-fashioned white Keds instead of the Naconas. and grabbed a gym-grey sweatshirt. The Colt fit snuggly into its chamois holster at the small of my back and the band of the sweatshirt covered it nicely. I tugged the shirt collar out of the sweatshirt's neck, rolled it halfway down and topped the ensemble off with a Seiko Mickey Mouse watch.

I waltzed to my drawing board and laid the four photographs across it and turned on the lamp. They were professional quality photographs, clear, not grainy, colors true. I didn't know much about photography, but the clarity suggested that these had been taken reasonably close to their target with

FROST

something other than a cellphone camera, and without a heavy telephoto lens to distort the imagery. Camey's face twisted into orgasmic bliss in all of them.

Pear's expression was one of simple, bland concentration. The positional variety indicated a certain time lapse between camera clicks, but Pear never seems to be climbing near the point of climax. I took a perverse satisfaction in that.

The doorbell bonged. I trotted to the front door, peered through the peephole.

"Mr. Frost?" A FedEx Courier offered an oversized cardboard envelope and an electronic clipboard. I scribbled *Frost* on the line and handed his board back.

The package held exactly what Chelsea had promised. An annual report put Pacific Investments' last year's gross income at just above twelve million dollars. Two majority stockholders were listed, together owning ninety-eight percent of the privately held corporation's stock. The other two percent was owned by something called Shelterville, an organization identified as a provider and maintainer of a number of shelters for minor-aged teenagers who found themselves on the streets.

A photocopy of a clipping from the Puget Sound Business Journal announced the acquisition of Pacific Investments by StoneVentures. The article broke down Pacific Investments product line, mentioned involvement in import and export, but offered no information on StoneVentures. Essentially, the package proved useless.

I flipped over the last page of Pacific Investments promotional material and found the Post-It note Chelsea had pasted to the center of the page. Her flowing, cursive script read *You are rapidly becoming the focus of my life.*

FROST

I shook my head and smiled.

***

A forest green 1976 Dodge Dart is probably not the logical choice for a stakeout, but I liked the car and besides, it was the only one I owned.

I paid some kid $2500 for it several years ago. The kid inherited the car from his grandmother--the original owner--in mint condition, but he wanted cash to buy a sporty little truck. He got his truck, I got a '76 Dart Custom with 78,000 original miles and a slant-six that would quickly climb to ninety miles an hour and hold it steadily enough to perch an uncovered cup of coffee on the dashboard without spilling any of it. The car was comfortable in an old fogey kind of way, too big, too green and ugly enough to blend into a crowded freeway provided nobody was looking for it.

I found Pear's name on one of those ancestry sites on the Internet. His home address was listed, and Camey Horne showed at the same address.

The house sat midway down West Lee in Queen Anne on the upward slope of a hill overlooking Puget Sound. I figured looking out of that picture window with a decent pair of binoculars you should be able to see everything from Bainbridge Island to Bellevue and back with Mounts Olympia and Rainier thrown in for good measure. I parked four houses down and across the street, turned off my car lights and sat.

I wasn't sure why I was here. Maybe whoever had fired the Nikon the first time would come back and I'd be able to collar him and slap him silly until he begged to answer my questions. Maybe I just needed to get out of the house and couldn't find a movie I

FROST

wanted to see.

Frankly, I didn't know what else to do. Pear and Camey were the only pieces of this puzzle I knew where to find, so I found them and hoped they might attract some of the other pieces.

I sat for almost an hour.

The lights inside the place turned off. Pear and Camey came out of the double front door and climbed into a red BMW. Both were dressed to kill, Pear looking like an overstuffed beach ball wrapped in a double-breasted tuxedo and Camey imitating a perfume ad in black sequined elegance. The car backed out of the driveway and drove off in the opposite direction.

I stayed in my car for another ten minutes to make certain no one had forgotten anything to warrant a return trip home. I grabbed a pair of cotton work gloves from under the front seat and climbed out of the Dodge.

The back bedroom window was opened halfway, presumably an attempt to allow a fresh air flow to the inside of the place. I popped the screen from the window, pulled it all the way open and climbed inside.

I had one of those little penlights the doctor uses to look inside your ears and your eyeballs. I didn't mean to steal it, but somehow two of them had wound up in my pocket during my last physical. I would've returned them, but both bore inscriptions for different pharmaceutical preparations, so I figured they probably hadn't cost the doctor anything and never got around to sending them back.

The inside of the house reeked of money, old money. Turn of the century antiques furnished the bedroom, a room almost large enough to hold the main floor of my entire house. A massive chest of drawers, hand-carved, hugged one corner and its

FROST

companion dresser sat against the adjacent wall. The mirror on the dresser was at least seven feet wide. A vintage oak vanity guarded another wall and a bed, apparently a made-to-specification item judging from the size, pressed into an octagonal platform nook. I stepped into the nook, sat on the bed and gazed at the ceiling.

Three light fixtures glared back at me, cold and hard metal things. I wondered briefly if Pear knew the middle one contained a camera lens. I stepped onto the bed and gingerly unscrewed the fixture. I debated whether or not to remove the thing's memory card, then remembered that I didn't really need any more graphic images of Pear and Camey grunting and groaning.

I crept out of the bedroom and down the hallway. Moonlight filled the cavernous living area, so I turned off the penlight and moved toward a massive oak rolltop desk. A quick glance yielded nothing of interest, but a foray into the bottom right hand drawer produced a leather bound loose-leaf address book the size of a paperback novel. I flipped to the *F* section and found my own name, address and unlisted telephone number scrawled halfway down the page. Five other entries followed my name, so I figured that unless Pear met five *F*s today, he'd known for some time that I lived in Seattle.

A plastic insert held half-a-dozen of Pear's business cards and a flashdrive. I palmed the address book and slithered into the kitchen. The refrigerator door held half a case of Henry Weinhard's Private Reserve. I took two bottles, stuffed them into an empty Starbuck's Coffee gift bag I found on the counter and tossed the address book in with them.

I took one last look at the expansive living room, realized the furniture in there was worth more money than I made last year. I shrugged, turned around and carried my bag out through the kitchen door.

The drive from Queen Anne back to West Seattle took almost twenty minutes. I parked the car at the curb and climbed the concrete steps that led to the front yard.

My stereo blared from behind the locked front door. I often left music turned on to keep my dog company, but never this loud and never set to pick up whatever station blasted rap lyrics against the walls of my living room.

I set the bag down on the tiny porch and retrieved the Colt from its pouch. I unlocked the bolt, turned the key in the doorknob and put the keys back into my pocket. Gently, I turned the doorknob and pushed open the door.

I stepped inside and punched the light switch. The room was empty. I pressed the power control button on the stereo and killed the noise, backed out the door, picked up the bag, stepped back inside and relocked the door.

I tossed the bag on the sofa.

Clutching the Colt, I swept through each room--the living room, both bedrooms, back porch--found no one, found nothing out of place. The only thing missing was my dog.

I stepped into the walkway that connected the kitchen to my bedroom and opened the basement door. I turned on the light switch, but darkness clung to the stairwell. Cursing under my breath, I grabbed the penlight from my pocket and slowly descended the blackened stairwell.

The flashlight beam glinted from the opened door to the breaker box. The circuit had been thrown, so I flipped it with the heel of my gun hand. Light flooded the basement.

Everything seemed to be just as I left it. I glanced around

FROST

the room a second time and then headed for the cubbyhole that served as a laundry room.

My dog's collar lay on top of the floor in front of the dryer. I felt my heart swell to three times its normal size and weight. I swallowed and opened the dryer door.

Crickett cowered on top of a load of still damp towels. She poked her furry ginger head out of the opening and whined.

I sat the Colt on top of the machine and picked her up. The dog trembled like a wino who'd sworn off sucking a bottle three days ago. I checked her over, ran my hands across her back, sides and belly, stroked her head looking for blood or broken bones. There were none.

Crickett burrowed her head into the belly of my sweatshirt. I found the dog while trying to recover several pieces of missing family jewelry for a client. Crickett was a filthy, skittish Llasa Apso chained inside the garage of my client's nephew, a punk who'd apparently swiped her not realizing there isn't much of a resale value for small stolen housepets. The dog barely whined when I'd opened the garage door. It hurt me to see the collapsed sides of her belly and I knew she wouldn't last much longer. The vet told me later she had two broken ribs, probably brought about by the toe of a workboot and a ruptured eardrum. The bozo who'd chained her made the mistake of kicking her as he stomped in my direction, then took a swing at me with a crowbar. I broke his arm in two places, and shattered his left kneecap. I left the crowbar crammed with all the force I could muster into the crotch of his greasy blue jeans.

The vet bill was almost a thousand dollars and I never did manage to find Crickett's original owner. She hadn't been chipped, and the truth is that I didn't look very hard.

FROST

I carried Crickett out of the laundry room. I noticed that the four photographs had been pulled off my drawing board and laid atop the adjacent taboret. An unfinished piece of art, an eighteen by twenty-four inch pencilled Rapunzel, now lay against the drawing surface. She was a proud beauty, naked save for a thin wisp of cloth wrapped around her full, sensuous body. Her long, thick hair tousled in an unseen breeze, wrapped delicately around slender shoulders.

Rapunzel had been violated. Half a bottle of Higgins Black Magic Ink covered the center of the picture, neatly obscuring her fiery eyes, her strong chin and most of the delicate detail introduced to render a child's story mate into a sensual fantasy. I'd spent almost nine hours working on the piece and now each and every one of those proud hours twisted into wasted moments.

Nothing else was damaged. Even the now empty ink bottle sat in its original perch neatly recapped on the top shelf of the taboret.

I picked up the photographs and carried Crickett upstairs. I laid her on the sofa and opened one of the Henry Weinhard's.

I laid the address book on the coffee table and began to scan it page by page. Crickett pressed herself against my thigh and fell asleep.

Pear was certainly not without influential contacts. I recognized the names of two United States Senators and a couple of West Coast Congressmen. The binder held two listings for each, a business address and a home address. The book also boasted a number of familiar business and civic leaders, and curiously a couple of big name entertainers: two popular actors, a recently chartbusting rock singer, a best-selling horror novelist, and a local news anchor.

FROST

I removed the plastic sheath from the notebook, pulled out Pear's business cards and placed one in my wallet. I tossed the others into the fireplace.

I fired up my laptop and plugged in the flashdrive, but the contents were password protected.

The house I rented had once been owned by dopers who used it as a marijuana nursery. One spot on the basement wall noted the number of plants and cuttings for a particular day. The growers had been right clever about building hidey-holes for harvested leaves and I went to one in the hall linen closet, opened it and dropped the address book inside. I replaced the shelf panel and straightened the towels.

Mickey told me it was just past midnight. I scooped up Crickett and carried her to bed, placed the Colt on the nightstand and laid down fully clothed on top of the comforter, then embraced a slumber filled with dreams of shattered fairy stories, vanished door locks and grinning fat men.

FROST

Chapter Four

Miles Stemper shook his head. "Any idea what's on this?" He tossed the flashdrive into the air and snatched it as if it were a flying insect.

"No."

Miles snorted, scratched the end of his nose with an index finger. "Finding the password on something like this is pretty much hit and miss."

I gazed at the monitor and winced. "I'd always heard you were the best there is at this sort of thing."

"Who in hell told you that?"

"You did."

"I lied."

"What do you recommend, Miles?"

Miles tapped the end of his nose with the same index finger. "I recommend you call Soprano's," he said, finally. "Tell 'em to bring me two extra-large extravaganzas minus the onions, thick crust. And two six packs of Pepsi, not those plastic bottles."

"Okay."

"And put in a tip for the delivery kid when you call. I'll let you know when and if I can get into this thing."

"Thanks. I owe you."

Miles paused. "You find things, right?"

"Sometimes."

"I've lost my car keys."

"You've lost your mind. You don't drive."

"Go. Get out. Leave me the hell alone to figure this out."

FROST

I made my way to the Java Bean, downed two cups of coffee and a couple of glazed doughnuts. I wondered for a moment if I should leave Crickett with someone for a few days, decided against it. If anybody was interested they'd come after me, not my dog.

I pulled out my laptop and signed into Standard & Poors, then the Thomas Register, and the Standard Directory of Advertisers. StoneVentures managed to abort coverage in all of them, could well be a hallucinatory company title pasted to an imaginary concoction of non-existent business activity.

Shelterville turned up in a Washington State Corporate directory as a non-profit subsidiary of something called StoneVentures.

I called a reporter friend at the Puget Sound Business Journal, but came up empty on StoneVentures and very close to empty on Pacific Investments, but he did point me toward a headquarter location for Shelterville, current Director of Operations being one Ned Lee.

The offices were located on the first floor of a two-story house up on Phinney Ridge. The place smelled of stale bread and iodine.

Lee was a rangy fellow, maybe six foot, thin with the pasty look of those who swear off ingesting red meat and never find a satisfactory substitute for the lost protein. He wore fashionably ragged Levi's, a Hawaiian print shirt and Birkenstock sandals. His steel grey hair brushed back, appeared short and trimmed until his head turned and a beak-nosed profile revealed a foot-long ponytail.

I introduced myself and flashed my license. "I appreciate you seeing me on such short notice."

FROST

"Not at all. I expected you to show up eventually."

"Excuse me?

"Well, not you in particular, but somebody working in your capacity."

"I tried not to look dumbfounded. "Well, then, Mr. Lee, why don't we save each other some time."

"Okay."

"Start from the beginning and don't worry about the formalities.   Of   course,   this   conversation   is   completely confidential.

"Sounds fair." Lee coughed. "As you know--"

"For the moment, let's pretend I don't know anything."

Lee bit his lower lip. "Six children have disappeared from our shelters in the last two months. Two of those were pregnant and expected to give birth at any time." He paused, looked down at his folded hands. "We have five shelters, Mr. Frost" He spread his hands in front of his face. "This is the only shelter not missing a charge."

"Could the kids have just walked away?"

Lee shook his head. "Unlikely. Most of the kids we deal with are put here by order of the courts. We don't lock them in, but we do lock the houses. Someone in authority is always on duty and always awake."

"What do the cops say?"

"They don't." Lee crossed his legs and began to absently tap his knee with the fingers of his left hand. "The police have more important matters to deal with," he spat. "These children are disposable."

"Disposable?"

FROST

"Most are runaways, with nobody looking for them. Some are petty criminals. Many have been involved in prostitution at one time or another. These kids are a nuisance, Mr. Frost, and the police just don't give a damn."

"I'll need copies of the files on the missing children."

"Of course."

"And a list of staffers at each location."

"When do you need that?"

I glanced at my watch and then turned what I hoped was an official looking stare toward Lee.

Lee took less than half-an-hour to compile the information. As I shook his hand I asked him what he knew about StoneVentures.

Lee frowned. "Who?"

"StoneVentures. They're the people who sign your paycheck."

"Oh. I really don't know anything about them. Shelterville was always a hand-to-mouth operation, then about two years ago we get this offer for corporate sponsorship. I changed the name on the Charter, took the money and ran."

"What do you think of Pearson Stone?"

"Never met him."

"Y'know, StoneVentures just bought an outfit here called Pacific Investments."

"Good. If they're buying other companies, they're healthy. If they're healthy, my bills get paid."

I nodded and smiled. "I appreciate your help, Mr. Lee."

"Anytime. Wish you luck."

***

FROST

Sam Rollins slid his bulk down into his chair and propped his feet up on the desk. "It's not on the department's Priority List, I can tell you that much."

"Why not?"

"C'mon, Micah. No evidence of foul play here. These kids came from the streets and there's nothing to suggest anything happened other than they went back to the streets."

"Can I see the files?"

"No."

"Why not?"

"Technically, those cases are still open."

"Who are they assigned to?"

"Greg Ahmann."

I guess my eyes rolled.

"He's a good cop."

"He's a putz, Sam."

"You're still pissed 'cause he shot you that once."

"I should've sued your ass off."

"You should've kept your ass out of the line of fire."

"Could you run a name for me, at least?"

"What name?"

"Pearson Stone."

"Why?"

"Because I said *please*?"

Sam shook his head. "I'll see what I can do. Any known aliases?"

I hesitated for a moment. "Pearson Frost. No relation."

***

FROST

I parked the Dodge at a meter in front of Aaron Brothers, bought a block of watercolor paper, then drove back to the house. The only message on my machine was a semi-pornographic teaser from Chelsea. I opened the back door so Crickett had access to the fenced backyard and carried the drawing paper downstairs to the basement.

I laid out a sheet of it, taped the corners with masking tape and measured off a two-inch border all around. Fortunately, I still had my preliminary sketches for Rapunzel. I fetched the compass from my drafting kit, rounded the inside of the corners and began sketching in the braided Celtic design that formed the picture's border.

Someone knocked at the upstairs front door. I turned off the high-intensity lamp on the drawing table and bounded up the stairs. The same courier from yesterday handed me a CD-sized package and an electronic clipboard. I signed off, thanked him, and closed the door.

I popped the packing tape off the thin box and opened the cardboard flap. There were four photographs inside.

The first was of Chelsea and me, taken yesterday at Cafe Sophie where we'd had a late lunch.

The second was of Chelsea decked out in a black leotard at her Barre class, probably the class she attended after we ate.

The third was of Chelsea sitting inside her glass-walled office at the employment agency she owned with her husband Charles.

The fourth was of Chelsea climbing out of the shower in her home, soaking wet and gloriously naked.

FROST

Chapter Five

"Do you shower in the evening before you go to bed or in the morning before you leave the house?"

Chelsea rolled her tongue across her lips. "That depends on what I have occasion to wash away."

"How about this morning?"

"Hot shower at six o'clock. Why?"

I reached inside my jacket pocket and produced the new batch of photographs. She pawed through them, then tossed them onto the table. "You didn't have to go to this much trouble. I would gladly have given you a guided tour."

"These were delivered to me at the house this afternoon."

"Who sent them?"

"I don't know."

"I want to know."

"Me, too. I want you to keep Crickett with you for a few days. She's small, but when she gets upset she's loud. Keep her with you all the time, at home and at work. Stay in crowds, stay with Charles. Send Kelly home from school with friends until you or Charles can pick her up."

"What are you going to do?"

"I have to see a man about some glossies."

"Yeah, well when you find him, punch his lights out."

"And I thought you were so demure."

"Son-of-a-bitch caught me before I'd put my makeup on."

I picked up the photos and gazed into the fourth one. "I hadn't noticed."

FROST

***

I parked the Dodge in virtually the same spot I used the night before. I checked my watch, noted five forty-five, and climbed out of the car.

I walked up the driveway to the front door and knocked, waited half-a-minute, knocked again. There was no answer. I trotted around to the back and let myself in through the same bedroom window. I wandered into the kitchen, pulled another Henry Weinhard's from Pear's private stock and sat myself down on a stool beside the kitchen counter.

Twenty minutes passed. I grabbed another beer from the fridge and an apple from a bowl on the counter. I pulled a small paring knife from a wooden butcher block, sliced off a bit of fruit and began to munch. I'd just opened the bottle when I heard the key turn in the lock. I wrapped my left hand around the bottle's neck, slipped the Colt out of its holster and turned toward the kitchen doorway.

Camey was alone. She came in, tossed her briefcase on the floor in front of the davenport and kicked off her shoes. I watched her slip out of her suit jacket, pull a white blouse out of the waistband of her skirt, then reach for the skirt's zipper.

"Would you like a beer?" I asked.

She glared across the room. "What are you doing here?"

"Where's your paramour?"

"San Francisco." She unzipped the skirt and stepped out of it. Camey didn't wear a slip. We watched each other for a moment, me in jeans and a pullover, she in a silk blouse and lace garters.

FROST

"There is scotch in the cabinet by the refrigerator. Half water, no ice."

FROST

Chapter Six

I mixed Camey's drink and carried it into the living room. Camey dropped onto the davenport and propped stockinged feet atop a cherry coffee table.

"What's in San Francisco?"

Camey took a long pull on the scotch. "A bridge. Hills. Several really good Chinese restaurants."

"And Pearson."

"Yes."

"What's he doing there? I mean, other than hopefully still limping."

She rolled her eyes toward me. "It's hard to believe you two are brothers."

"I've always had a hard time believing it."

She pulled at the drink again. "How'd the two of you learn to hate each other so much?"

"Years of practice."

Camey set the empty glass on the coffee table. "What is it you want, exactly, Micah Frost?"

"I want to be left alone."

Camey shook her head. "That's why you break into houses, I suppose."

"That's just a hobby."

She nodded toward her empty glass. "Get me another, will you? Less water."

I mixed the drink and handed it to her, sat down again. Camey put the glass on the floor and twisted, placed her head on

FROST

the arm of the davenport and her legs across my lap. I perched for a moment, wondered what to do with my hands. Finally, I wrapped my left hand around the beer and laid my right hand just above her ankle.

"You've got nice hands," she said.

"How long have you known Pear?"

"Seven years. How long have you been brothers?"

I pursed my lips, felt my eyes glaze over...

"Kill it."

"No." A hardboned fist slammed into the boy's cheek. He hit the ground, gasped for breath.

The dog scurried to the fallen child and licked his face. the boy rolled on top of the black and white animal, firmly cuddled the creature beneath his chest.

The pistol dangled from the man's hand, glinted in the evening sun. He brushed an imaginary speck of dust from the sleeve of his uniform, then snarled, "Get up."

The fat boy watched from behind his father, eyes wide, a stupid grin carved into round, ruddy cheeks. "Let me kill it, Dad."

The uniformed man handed the pistol to the fat boy. "Watch your aim, boy. Micah, get away from the goddamned dog."

The seven-year-old gritted his teeth. "Go to Hell, old man."

A military boot slammed into the boy's stomach. The puppy scampered as the boy fought to get up, feet scrambled in the dust, and he fell, pushed himself up, slipped in the dry scum.

FROST

The fat boy raised the pistol with both hands, bent his knees, his posture a perfect example of a military target shoot. His sibling grabbed a handful of dry dirt and threw it into the fat boy's grinning faced, then leapt toward him.

The fat boy fired blind...

I looked at the purplish scar above my left wrist. "We were never brothers."

Camey looked at me a long time, brown eyes glistening in the soft evening light. "He scares you."

I looked at her, said nothing.

"He scares me, too."

"Why do you stay?"

"Money, I suppose, has a lot to do with it."

"Hmmm."

Her soft eyes hardened into metal orbs. "Ever been broke, Frost?"

"Most of my life."

"I mean really, completely broke. On the street, nowhere to go, no one gives a flip, I'll fuck-you-for-a-hamburger broke."

"No."

"I have." Camey picked up her drink, slurped at the ginger-colored mixture. "I left home at fourteen. Old story, stepdad thought the marriage vows included me as well as mom. Wouldn't stay out of my room, wouldn't get out of my bed, until--well, anyway, mom didn't believe me and I left. I spent the next two years on the streets, two long, hard years." She paused, then added, "Hard in more ways than one.

39

FROST

"So, I'm in a Denny's one night about three in the morning and this guy walks in with two of his pals. Pudgy, but powerful looking, not the kind of guy you'd want to mess with. One of the guys starts to hit on me and I told him to shove off."

Camey's eyes glazed. "I pushed him away. He backed over--something, I don't know. Anyway, he tripped, fell on his butt. The place was almost empty, but everybody who was there started laughing at the guy.

"He was mad. I'd seen mad lots of times and I didn't like it. He climbed off the floor and grabbed me, slapped once, hard. I saw his hand close into a fist.

"Pear was on him like grease on bacon. This guy was a big man, tall, and strong. He looked like one of those body builders, but it didn't matter. Pear doubled him over, slammed his head into the counter and yanked me out of there and into his car.

"We were driving into the night and he looked me over, asked if I was okay. He apologized for his friend's behavior, never tried to excuse the guy, just said he was sorry for interrupting my meal and that if I was still hungry he knew a great little place for breakfast. The car was warm and dry, and the offer of food without having to fuck for it was too good a deal to pass up.

"Pear drove to this really upscale place, parked the car, and took my arm. I was hesitant, but he seemed unconcerned about my street appearance. We walked in and some guy in a suit ran up to him, told him how good it was to see him again, hustled us over to what had to be the best table in the place.

"The guy asked *me* if the seating was satisfactory. Me, not Pear.

"Pear didn't talk so much as listen while we ate. No one had taken the time to care about what I had to say for so very, very

40

FROST

long. I talked through the night and well into the morning. Pear said he had something he wanted to show me, drove me back to his house. I thought, well, here it comes, but he took me inside, put me in a bedroom with a private bath and told me to get some sleep.

"I slept through most of the afternoon. When I woke up, my grungy clothes were gone, and new clothes and a pair of new shoes had been left for me. I got up, showered, put on the new clothes and wandered out looking for Pear.

"Pear introduced me to the maid as a friend who would be staying for a while, then took me shopping. And not to Sears.

"He spent about fifteen thousand dollars on me that afternoon. Fun stuff, jeans, shirts, boots, but serious stuff, too. There were a couple of business suits, some evening clothes, high-heels. He took me to a styling salon and they worked me over, did my hair, my nails and showed me how to use makeup.

"When it was all done, Pear took me into another restaurant and ordered dinner for us. He asked me if I'd like to work with him. Not for him, with him. He said he needed someone who had a lot on the ball and wanted to learn. He'd send me to school part-time, I'd work as his assistant. I'd stay at his house and he'd give me two thousand dollars a month spending money.

"He said sleeping with him wasn't part of the job."

Camey slid down on the davenport, pressed her butt against my thigh. "He brought in private tutors and put me to work. My whole world changed in a single night.

"Pear was terrific. He expected me to be available for business activities, but if he wanted to spend time with me otherwise he always asked, like a date. He was always a perfect gentleman. It took months for him to kiss me.

"I moved into his room shortly after that.

"Pear began to change. He became more demanding, at the office and in bed. I realized that some of his business dealings weren't strictly legitimate, but by that time it was too late. Pear owned me."

I moved my hand gently, brushed the soft, tanned flesh along her inner thigh. "Nobody owns you, Camey."

She pulled up the hem of the blouse. A brutal three-inch scar rippled across the otherwise smooth skin on her tummy. Her eyes blinked, teared up. "I tried to leave, once." Camey stroked my hand and pulled it to her breast.

"Camey..."

"Let me make my own decisions." She unbuttoned two buttons and pushed my hand inside the white silk blouse. My fingers found the front clasp of a bra and unclipped the garment. Camey flexed and the bra fell away beneath the blouse. My hand found a full breast and stroked gently.

Camey put her hand on top of mine, pressed it against her and rolled to the floor. She kneeled in front of me, pressed her cheek against the soft denim covering my thigh, then moved toward me and lightly kissed the denim below my navel.

Camey gazed at me, smiled, and undid my jeans. she rubbed her lips against my belly, slid her hand inside my jeans. I lifted up, she tugged the jeans away and I felt her tongue, then the warmth of her mouth around me.

***

FROST

Stars filled the night sky, points of light frozen like a fireworks display somehow stopped mid-explosion. I took a long look at the unclothed woman draped across the Persian carpet. Camey dozed, gently snoring. I thought to cover her, realized how warm the night was.

I retrieved my jeans, pulled them on, and stepped into my white Keds.

Camey stirred. "Micah?"

"I'm here, Camey."

"Can you stay?"

I thought of the camera hidden above the bed. "Come with me."

Camey rolled onto her tummy. Moonlight played against the soft flesh across her back and bottom, wrapped her in a haloed glow. "Want to take me to dinner?"

"I could do that."

"Help me up."

Camey stretched a hand toward me and I pulled. She pushed into the tug and pressed against my naked chest. "How hungry are you?" I asked.

"Very." she pulled away slightly, rubbed erect nipples against my chest. "I'll get dressed."

I watched Camey paddle across the hardwood floor toward the bedroom and vanish through the doorway. She reappeared moments later wearing white jeans, a navy blue cotton pullover and white sneakers. Her thick auburn hair pulled back into a simple ponytail. She'd touched up red lipstick, slipped on a black sports watch, and pulled on red horn-rim glasses. "My contacts are soaking and my eyes are tired," she explained.

FROST

Camey was lovely. The casual clothes somehow emphasized her beauty, the spectacles made her more human, more touchable. She grabbed her purse. "Where can we get a good cheeseburger?"

I drove into Ballard, headed toward the Locks. Camey sat next to me on the Dart's bench seat, wrapped a hand inside my thigh and laid her head on my shoulder. I pulled into an empty space and we walked into the Lockspot Cafe. We found a table away from the bar. I sat facing the door.

"Order for me," she said when the waitress arrived. I ordered bacon cheeseburgers, fries and coffee for both of us.

Camey took my hand in both of hers and moved her chair closer to mine. She talked, about books and music, expressed a preference for Michael Moorcock and George Winston. She adored the subtle sensuality of Steve Hanks' watercolors, loved the silly seriousness of the old operatic Mighty Mouse cartoons, hated asparagus, raisins and green beans, would fight an angry horde for fried chicken and barbeque potato chips. The food arrived, finally, and Camey devoured her cheeseburger .

Then, she burped.

"Excuse me," she giggled. All semblance of the corporate matriarch had vanished, replaced by a fresh-faced twenty-four year old playful girl who stroked my hand and licked my ear.

"You're amazing," I said.

"How do you mean?"

"Without the uniform you're almost likeable."

She dipped her head. "Thank you, kind sir. The question now is what are you going to do with me?"

"What did you have in mind?"

"You could keep me."

44

FROST

I tossed a couple of twenty dollar bills on the table and we left the bar, my hand around Camey's waist, her arm around my shoulders. It felt good.

I opened the car door and Camey slid to the middle of the bench seat. I climbed in beside her and popped the key into the ignition switch. I drove to Gasworks Park on Lake Union and parked. The night was warm, almost muggy. We found a small hill overlooking the lake and lay on damp grass and watched a small boat chug across the water.

"What about Pear?"

Camey lay against my chest, silent for a time. "I can't handle him," she said, finally, "but I think we could."

"Camey..."

"I feel safe with you."

I pulled her close, wrapped my arms around her. I held her for long time, smelling her hair, stroking the small of her back.

The night ebbed away as dawn crept toward us from the east. We walked to the Dart and I drove her back to her house on Queen Anne. She pulled me inside and we made love desperately, fully dressed, clothing askew, Camey bent over the kitchen counter, her fingers gripping the counter's edge, her smooth, firm bottom slamming into me, my hands shoved under the navy pullover cupping her unfettered breasts, until, finally, she climaxed, screaming, squirming, pulling me inside until I thought I might disappear into her, then wriggled and pushed and quivered and came again, and this time so did I.

She cried, softly.

I held her for a time, tried to convince her to leave with me. She needed to pack and put a few things in order, she said. I promised to pick her up at one o'clock.

FROST

I took the slow road home, cruised along Pike's Market and Pioneer Square. The sun was fully into the sky now, bright, bathing the city in its cleansing beams. My eyes eclipsed the dirt and the clutter, found only architectural triumph, the Seattle cityscape warm and inviting. I parked the car at a meter on First Avenue and walked into Starbucks, ordered black coffee and two glazed doughnuts.

I watched the commuters from the window for a while, men mostly in suits and ties, women in skirts and tennis shoes. I thought about Camey, wished I'd pulled the memory card from the fixture above her bed. I'd get it this afternoon and destroy it.

I drove home, showered, pulled on fresh clothing--jeans and a cotton crewneck sweater--and slipped back into the sneakers. It dawned on me that lately I'd worn the boots less and less.

There was nothing on my voicemail. I glanced at my watch, saw I had three hours before meeting Camey.

The same courier knocked on my front door and offered another small package. I checked for a return address, but there was none.

I closed the door and opened the box. Four more photographs lay inside. The first was of me sitting alone in the kitchen at Camey's Queen Anne house holding a beer bottle. The second was of Camey and me on the davenport in the living room, her undraped legs across my lap. The third showed Camey on her knees in front of me, a hand on each of my legs with her head on my thigh. The fourth showed Camey folded over a kitchen counter, clothing twisted, her hands grasping the edge of the counter as I took her from behind.

FROST

I stormed into the kitchen and threw the photos on top of the microwave. I picked up the memo pad I'd used to record Pear's home address and telephone number and punched the number into the pad on the wall phone.

It rang twice, then picked up. "Hello," a male voice said.

"Who is this?"

"Detective Sam Rollins, Seattle Police. Who is this?"

FROST

Chapter Seven

I drove to Queen Anne and turned onto West Lee.

A half-dozen patrol cars sat in the driveway. I pulled alongside the house and glanced around looking for Sam Rollins.

Sam found me first. He gazed long and hard as I stepped out of the car. He waited, hands inside his trouser pockets, arms framing a bulk of stomach as he stood.

"Sam."

"Micah."

"What's going on?"

"I was hoping you could tell me."

"Is Camey Horne inside?"

Sam nodded. I started toward the house and Sam grabbed my arm. "You don't want to go in there."

My weight sank down around my ankles. I felt a blast of warmth, knew I was falling. Sam grabbed me, eased me to a seat on the driveway curb.

"How do you know the girl?"

I tried to swallow, my throat suddenly dry and my tongue seemingly twice its normal size. I tried to take a deep breath, but the air stuck in my throat.

Sam reached into his jacket pocket and produced a thin handful of photographs. "I scooped these out of a desk drawer. I need to know what this is all about."

"Me, too," I wheezed. "I'll tell you what I know, but not here, not now. I can't."

FROST

Sam glanced at his watch. "Bookstore, Micah, five o'clock." I nodded, then climbed unsteadily to my feet. "If you aren't there, every cop in the city will be looking for your butt."

"I'll be there." I took a deep breath, tried to steady myself as I walked to my car. It took several tries to fit the key into the ignition, but the Dart fired at once. I drove away, stopped four blocks down the street, opened the car door and puked.

***

I drove aimlessly for hours. Three-thirty found me on the south end of Tacoma heading west toward Gig Harbor. I knew if I was to have any chance of making a five o'clock meeting in downtown Seattle I'd best turn around.

I fought the rush hour traffic, finally pulled into the parking garage at Pacific Place and made my way to the cafe inside Barnes & Noble. Sam Rollins was already there, seated at a table against the far corner. I shuffled over and sat across from him.

"You look like shit, Frost."

I rubbed a hand across my face. "How'd it happen?"

"Slowly and with a great deal of pain. Somebody literally nailed the girl's hands to the kitchen counter, wrapped her mouth with duct tape and disemboweled her."

I choked down bile.

"All of it, Micah. Now."

I started talking. I told Sam everything that had happened from the moment Camey showed up at my front door to my promise to pick her up this afternoon.

"Why didn't you tell me Stone was your brother?"

"I don't think of him as my brother."

49

FROST

"But Camey Horne knew."

"Yes."

"Who else?"

I shrugged. "I don't know, Sam. Somebody must, but I'll be damned if I know who."

"I've got to ask, Micah. Where were you between seven and eight this morning?"

"Java Bean in Ballard. The barista there is named Charlotte, she'll verify it."

Sam produced a small leather bound notebook, scribbled into it. "Have you spoken to Stone?"

"He's in San Francisco."

Sam frowned. "Where'd you hear that?"

"From Camey."

Sam rubbed at his left eye with a massive fist. "Stone is in Seattle, never left. Says he was in his office at six this morning. There's a passkey system in the building, works in conjunction with a numerical password. The log shows him checking in a little before six. Security in the lobby says he was the first one in this morning."

"He could have gone back out."

"Maybe, but the Security guy doesn't remember him leaving, and the electronics don't show him punching back in. He couldn't access his office without carding it."

"I walked into his offices the other day and I didn't have to punch any buttons."

"The system releases at nine in the morning, locks back in at five. Business hours, you don't need to click in."

"Pear could have left and come back after nine."

FROST

"The reception came in at seven-thirty, says Stone was in his office."

"Dolly?"

Sam twisted his features into a grimace. "The receptionist is a Michelle something or other. "Who's Dolly?"

I shook my head. "Did you run Stone?"

"Yeah. Nothing there." Sam reached into his jacket pocket and produced four photographs. I glanced through them, copies of those delivered to me this morning. "I'd lose those if I were you."

I nodded. "Thanks, Sam."

"And Micah--stay away from this. Let us handle it."

"Okay."

"Right."

FROST

Chapter Eight

An empty house will echo even a sneakered footstep. I filled the house with echoes, pushed the sounds into corners and closets, pounded the hardwood floor until the buffed surface scuffed and smeared and smacked when I touched it.

I gazed at the photographs of Camey and me for the hundredth time, washed out the detail, focused on her beautiful face. Life, I think, is a string of possibilities and I mourned the loss of this special possibility, for the senseless end of a young life, for the loss of a promise, of immediate hope, of impending fulfillment.

Camey came to me in anger, turned to me in need, trusted me in loneliness, sought to embrace the oneness we all seek.

Camey Horne was dead.

The sun broke over the horizon in the east. I pulled off my clothing and stumbled to the bathroom, turned on the shower and adjusted the water to as high a temperature as I could stand. I washed, scuffed my skin with a battered hand brush, scraped away dirt and sweat. I scrubbed my hair twice, inhaled the sickly sweet scent of papaya shampoo and allowed the scalding water to rinse away the touch of yesterday.

I began turning off the hot water in small increments, allowed myself to briefly acclimate to the cold, turned the spigot to make it colder. In a few moments I stood naked under a burst of liquid frigidity. My teeth began to chatter, but I stood, silent and still until the flesh on my arms and legs changed to a purplish hue.

FROST

I began to scream, screamed into the icy blast of the water. The sound twisted into a gurgling howl, most of the volume lost amidst the cold cascade, but I screamed long and hard and with all my being. Finally, I turned off the water, toweled dry and looked into the mirror.

Wet white hair smiled back from beneath the brown. The broken nose curved slightly to the left above the mustache, and the jawline lacked the firmness held in years gone by. The eyes peered from beneath thick eyebrows, grey flecked with green, smaller than I might have preferred.

Even to me the eyes seemed cold and distant. I could be charming and helpful and sympathetic and completely uninvolved, all at the same time, which is probably why at forty years old I was a single man living alone with an eccentric Llasa Apso.

I closed my eyes and felt Camey's touch, felt her fingers along my cheek, felt her lips against my own, felt the warmth inside myself as I again heard her voice. I savored the possibility.

I opened my eyes and found my own reflection in the steamed mirror, alone.

Camey Horne was dead. Micah Frost was alive, damned alive.

And damned angry.

FROST

Chapter Nine

"Pacific Investment."

"Good morning, Michelle. Please put me through to Pearson Stone."

"May I tell him who's calling?"

"His brother."

Jim Brickman played soft piano while I waited on hold.

"Micah, this is Pear. What do you want?"

"Meet me at the Bay Cafe at Fisherman's Terminal, eleven o'clock."

There was a long pause. "This isn't a good day for me."

"This isn't a good day for either of us."

"I'm not sure I can make it."

"Do yourself a favor, Pear, and make it."

"That sounds distinctly like a threat, Micah."

"How very perceptive."

***

The Bay Cafe looked a cross between Pop's Soda Shoppe and the cafeteria from an old Star Trek rerun, resplendent in linoleum wood veneer and retro-blue vinyl, but the food was good and the view overlooking the combination commercial and pleasure boat marina offered an agreeable and very public venue.

The hostess showed me to a table in the back corner. The daily lunch crowd would begin to trickle in around noon and pack the place by twelve-thirty, but I hoped to be gone by then.

FROST

Pear marched through the doorway, pulled off Ray Ban sunglasses, and glanced around the room. He'd wrapped his bulk in a purple and white athletic suit, one of those plastic zippered things with Nike scrawled across the chest, the back, both arms and one leg. He left the Ray Bans dangling from a cord around his neck. Pear found my table and stomped toward me, waving off the hostess as he moved.

"This better be good," Pear said, plopping into a straight-backed wooden chair. The waitress brought menus and I ordered two coffees.

"I'm here," Pear said. "Tell me why."

"What are you doing in Seattle?"

"None of your fucking business. I don't answer to you."

I took a deep breath, chose my words carefully. "Pear, I couldn't care less about what you do as long as it doesn't affect me, but that isn't the case right now. I want to know who sent the pictures. I want to know who sent those emails with my contact information. I want to know who broke into my house and I want to know who photographed my friend."

Pear snorted. "Which friend?"

"Both of them."

Pear reached into the inside pocket of the Nike jacket, recovered a handful of photographs and slapped them on the table, photos of Camey, Chelsea and Kelly in various stages of undress.

The waitress stepped up with a steaming pot of fresh coffee, glanced at the table and gasped. I drummed my fingers on the wooden veneer and smiled at her. "My brother's new hobby."

The waitress grinned. "Nice work." She refilled the cups and walked away.

FROST

"Camey said she tried to leave you a couple of years ago. Said you stopped her, showed me a scar."

Pear picked up his mug and sipped at the coffee, apparently unphazed. "Yeah, I kept her under lock and key. That's why you had so much trouble finding an opportunity to fuck her."

"None of this bothers you, does it?"

Pear shrugged, round shoulders rolled against his plastic jacket. "Women come, women go. I don't get attached."

"Those photographs Camey showed me suggest more than just a casual friendship."

"There was a certain--convenience?--sex has very little to do with love, Micah."

"Tell me about her."

"Fuck you."

The waitress ambled back over to the table. "Did you boys want to order food?"

Pear stood up. "I think we're done here." He turned toward the waitress and asked her name.

"Dawn," she said.

"Dawn, have you ever done any modeling?"

***

I punched six snapshots onto the bulletin board mounted on the far wall of the basement, six children frozen in time, frozen in motion. I scanned the jackets again, verified no real commonality between them--save pregnancy for two of the girls-- and the fact that all were runaways below the age of sixteen.

FROST

I tromped upstairs to the linen closet and retrieved Pear's leather bound address book. I took the thing downstairs, poured yet another cup of coffee and began to prowl through the listings.

About a third of the names registered with a small black dot, seemingly incidental, but definitely present, between the first and last names. The names I recognized were a mix of business and entertainment professionals, and most bore a West Coast address. I couldn't imagine what the marked names shared, other than a listing in Pear's book.

I retrieved my scanner, plugged it into my laptop and spent the next hour scanning the entire book, then saving two copies on separate flashdrives. If my prowler returned and found Pear's book I'd still have access to the contents.

I called Miles. He'd had no luck breaking into the flashdrive I'd left him. He'd set up a system to input a random sequence of potential entry codes based on some sort of algebraic equation I couldn't possibly hope to understand. Miles promised to call if and when.

All I could do was wait.

I missed Crickett at my feet. I climbed into the chair at the art table and out of habit pulled my feet beneath my chair so the little dog had room to crawl into the space between the table's support brackets where she generally slept while I worked. I knew she was safer away from the house, but that didn't help.

I worked over the braided Celtic design on the corners of the piece, firmed up the line work and erased the guide marks.

I glanced at my watch, almost noon. I pushed away from the drawing table and headed up the stairs.

FROST

Today felt more like Autumn, cooler, heavy grey clouds filling the sky. I tucked the Colt inside my jeans and pulled on a soft suede sports jacket.

The Dart fired up. I pointed it toward the West Seattle Bridge and rolled away.

I got lucky, found a meter a block away from the parking garage exit at the Columbia Tower. Chelsea chatted up Dolly Michelle Parton and learned Pear had a one o'clock lunch appointment.

I tucked my credit card into the parking register, then slid back in behind the wheel. Ten minutes later, Pear pulled away in the red Beemer, headed toward First Avenue. I eased into traffic, merged with the flow. Pear crossed First Avenue and headed south, turned off at the West Seattle Bridge. I wondered for a moment if he meant to find his way to my place, but he turned off at Admiral Way, drove to California Avenue and parked across from Angelina's. I watched him ooze out of the Beemer and slither into the restaurant.

I parked curbside down the block, out of sight of Angelina's front door, I hoped, and waited almost forty minutes. Pear came out followed by a blonde youngster, maybe twenty years old, hair hanging limply to the middle of his back and skinned just above the ear on each side. Skin tight white jeans and a black motorcycle jacket were a sharp contrast to Pear's generously cut Italian suit.

The pair shook hands. Pear started toward the BMW, the kid in the opposite direction. I tapped my finger against the steering wheel, remembered that I knew where to find Pear and followed the kid.

FROST

Blondie didn't go very far. He climbed onto an older Yamaha motorcycle, pulled on a helmet and gunned toward Alki Beach.

The kid turned onto Halleck Avenue, fired up the hill onto the sharply sloped driveway of a four story monstrosity. The outside wall boasted a finish of blanched timber wrapped around a wide picture window at every level. Looking up, I could see oak beams across the ceilings. The house was ugly, but clean, the yard well kept.

Two teenaged faces stared at the beach from the top floor. Both were female. One stood up and I saw she was topless. She pressed against the window, budding breasts mashed against plated glass, then jerked away.

Blondie now stood with his back against the window. I tugged a notepad out of my inside jacket pocket, jotted down the address and the license number on the bike's tag. Two other cars, an old Maverick and a late model Bronco, also sat in the driveway. I noted tag numbers, waited half an hour, got bored and left.

Five o'clock found me in the same downtown parking spot. Pear left the garage several minutes later and drove to the house on West Lee. I parked and sat.

Pear stepped outside two hours later wearing khaki slacks and a white cardigan over a pink golf shirt. He drove to Shilshole and disappeared into Ray's Boathouse.

An hour passed. I hadn't eaten since this morning and I needed to pee, so I finally thought to Hell with it, opened the door to the Dart and headed into the restaurant.

I walked out of the men's room and into the bar, ordered a Comfort & Coffee and a Bacon Cheeseburger.

FROST

Pear sat against the far wall with a distinguished looking middle-aged man who looked somehow familiar, but I couldn't place him. Pear produced a leather satchel, handed it to the man unopened. The two men shook hands, smiled, and the man whose name refused to leave the tip of my tongue sashayed out of the bar not realized I'd snapped his picture with my cellphone.

Pear sat for a while. Eventually, a buxom young lady entered the bar and approached his table, caressed his pudgy shoulder and slid in next to him.

I shook my head, paid the check, and left.

***

"Tell me about Michelle."

Chelsea laughed into the phone. "Aside from the obvious, what would you like to know?"

"For starters, how long she's had a personal relationship with Pearson Stone."

Silence, then, "Are you serious?"

"Very."

"You're sure?"

"Saw them at Ray's Boathouse last night in the bar."

"Could have been business."

"Maybe, but the last thing I'd want at a business conference is Miss Parton without a bra."

"You're kidding--"

"Nope. They're all her's."

"Maybe, but I'll bet they were bought and paid for."

"I don't think so, not from the way they moved."

"Excuse me?"

60

FROST

"I'm an artist, you know. I've had years of intense hands-on study."

"You in the mood for homework?"

"What can you tell me about her?"

Michelle Grant, Chelsea told me, lived in an apartment on Sunnydale in Wallingford. She was twenty years old, unmarried, unchilded, with two years of Community College. She earned a living in a department store until she grew weary of working nights, weekends and holidays, and then she worked as a temp for Chelsea for the last seven months. Michelle spent the last two months at Pacific Investment.

"Did Stone specifically request Michelle or did you just send her based on qualifications?"

"Stone interviewed a dozen girls, told me he wanted Michelle. I doubt he knew her before the interview."

"Has she ever been in any kind of trouble?"

"Michelle's bonded through us, like all of my other girls. Any trouble with the law would've shown up on the background check." Chelsea paused. "Should I talk to her?"

"No."

"I don't like the girls dating the clients, Micah. It can lead to some real problems."

"I can imagine."

"No, you can't, even though you think you can."

"How's my dog?"

"Loud. She barks at everything."

"Good, that's her job."

"And I think she misses you. Want to speak to her?"

I heard Chelsea call my dog, heard the animal grunt in the distance. "Crickett? This is dad. How're ya doin' ?"

FROST

"Urr-arrrfff!!!"
"See you soon, sweetheart."
"Urr-arrrfff!"
"Goodbye, honey."
"Goodbye yourself, honey."

***

Pacific Investment owned the Halleck House, acquired it a couple of months ago. The title transfer showed no lien holders, indicating a cash purchase price of $620,000.00. Out of curiosity, I ran the house on West Lee, found identical information and a cash purchase price of neatly two-and-a-half million bucks.

Pear apparently did *very* well.

I punched the remote control and the television blared to life, settled in to watch the news, but the phone rang.

"Micah? Sam."

"Actually, my last name is Frost, not Sam."

"Wiseass. The bike is registered to a David Welsh. It's a new number converted from a California license two months ago."

"Surprise, surprise."

"Speaking of surprises, are you sure about the number on the Bronk?"

"Yep."

"Well, this gets kind of interesting."

"How so?"

"The Maverick belongs to Shelterville."

"Okay."

"Guess who owns the Bronco?"

62

FROST

The television screen flickered the *News at Noon* logo. A distinguished looking middle-aged man appeared on the screen, his name stamped in white letters across the bottom.

"Steven Cook," I murmured.

FROST

Chapter Ten

I met Miles at La Cocina a little before five. He'd grabbed a table by the open glass front of the place and sat slurping a gigantic margarita. I approached the table and he raised his hand, snapped his fingers and waved a peace sign at a waiter. I flashed the same gesture.

Miles watched two women on the sidewalk across the street. The held hands and giggled, kissed each other on the cheek, patted each other's bottoms, blended perfectly into the Friday evening Broadway street crowd.

"Ah, young love," I said, climbing into my chair.

"Ever been married, Micah?"

I felt my eyes fold over. "Yeah."

"I can't seem to picture you as a husband."

'That's probably because I'm not gay."

Miles laughed, rubbed his chin. "What happened?"

"She died."

"I'm sorry."

"Long time ago."

"I was married, once."

"What happened?"

Miles stretched his lips into a smirk and then blew me a kiss across the table. "Take a wild guess."

The waiter brought four margaritas. He sat two in front of me, two in front of Miles. We both ordered broiled chicken, rice, beans and flour tortillas.

FROST

Miles chatted about everything and nothing. The food came and he talked as he ate, eventually ordered flan for both of us, talked some more. I listened, grunted where it seemed appropriate.

The waiter cleared the empty plates and brought coffee. Miles reached under the table and pulled out a soft leather portfolio. "Who is this Stone guy?"

"Long, dull story."

"Long maybe, dull I doubt. I broke into the flashdrive." Miles pulled a notebook computer out of the portfolio, tapped the screen and it flickered to life. Then, he handed me a flashdrive I'd never seen before. "Be careful with that, most of it can get us arrested."

I grinned. "Okay."

"I'm serious."

The disk held an extensive array of crisp jpegs, shot after shot after shot of adult men coupling with very young partners. I scanned past the photos to what appeared to be an accounting ledger, each entry coded to a particular array of jpegs--dozens of photos, often of the same man slamming different adolescent partners--accompanied by dates and dollar figures and some kind of numerical code.

"Whoever put this together is a real slug," Miles said.

I nodded. "What are these numerical sequences, bank accounts?"

"Looks like it. The numbers are jumbled, and I can straighten that out, but the problem is that they're all partials. The account numbers are there, but the institution numbers are missing."

"Excuse me?"

FROST

"Every financial institution in the country, well, in the world for that matter, has a numerical locator code on the front end of the account number it assigns to its customers. Without that code there's no way of knowing which of the literally thousands of issuers these accounts reside in."

"You don't know which banks the accounts are in."

"Bingo."

"Did you look for some kind of hidden--"

"Do try not to insult me, Micah."

"Did you happen to add--"

"There are over two thousand names on that ledger, Micah, and better than thirty million dollars in deposits, as of last Thursday, anyway."

"Blackmail?"

"I'm not sure. There's a large initial deposit, and then a number of the entries show continuing payments made at regular intervals, like an installment payment plan. It looks like this maybe starts as blackmail and then continues as a provided service."

I felt sick to my stomach. "Anything on the drive to tie this to Stone?"

"Not a damned thing, other than the fact that you stole it from his house which makes it inadmissible evidence even if there were something to tie it to him. Stone probably has institution and access codes tucked away on another flashdrive. If you can find that we might be able to tie him to it."

I glanced at my watch. "Almost six-thirty. I guess I'll have to try and get that flashdrive. You up for breaking into another one?"

FROST

"Sure.   Most people use the same entry code on every locked drive they access, speaking of which, I think you'll get a kick out of the password on this one."

"What is it?"

"*F-R-O-S-T.*"

FROST

Chapter Eleven

She was easy to find, assuming one knew how to identify the tiny differences between the actual and the cosmetic.

Her jeans were skintight, worn and thin, just like the other girls on the avenue, but the knees in her denim trousers held their shape, the cloth still complete, untattered and unscuffed. Real working girls spend most of the work night kneeling, often in cobbled alleyways or the darkened paved corners of parking lots and the knees on their jeans wear out quickly if the girl is reasonably attractive and at least moderately ambitious.

Suede cowboy boots peeked from beneath the denim trousers, the heels and toes squared and whole, no tears, no rough scrapes or smears on the nap of the uncut leather. These were boots unaccustomed to the slashes of pavement hooks and concrete blemishes.

The makeup was a bit strong, but evenly applied, not the light toss and splatter approach used by a girl who'd spend her evening rubbing her cheeks against the trousered thigh of a paying stranger. Cosmetic smears on pants legs make for an unhappy customer and no working girl wants to deal with an aggravated mark.

She leaned against the wall of the Deja Vu Strip Club, one hand toying with the tassel of a tied leather belt, the other hidden beneath the bolds of a white poet's blouse. I walked up and smiled. "Having any luck?"

She looked at me with cold eyes. "I'm waiting for a friend."

"Actually, a friend sent me."

FROST

"Who's that?"

"Miles Stemper."

"Are you Michael Frost?"

"Micah."

"Like the rock."

"Like the rock."

"Sorry." She shoved her right hand toward me. "Donna Trent."

"Like the coat?"

"Trent, not Trench." Her eyes flashed. "So, *Michael*, want to buy a girl--" she paused, "--dinner?"

"I don't know. Are you a good date?"

"Best you can buy."

"Do you like seafood?"

"Hate it."

"Good. How about something red and bleeding?"

"I'll bite."

"I'll bet."

Donna cocked her head, peered at me from the corner of her eyes. "You're not as big as Miles led me to believe."

I arched my eyebrows. "How can you tell?"

We walked up Pike to Second Avenue, heeled left past Union and into the Metropolitan Grill. The waiter guided us to a back booth and Donna ordered drinks for both of us. The waiter vanished, returned momentarily with two glass vats filled half and half with Southern Comfort and iced water. "Are you ready to order?" he asked.

I hadn't seen a menu yet.

"Oh, I think so," Donna said.

"Uh..."

FROST

"I'll have the New York Strip, hefty cut, medium rare with French fries, no salad. Tomato bisque to start, apple cobbler to finish."

"Hungry?" I asked.

"The gentleman with the Mickey Mouse watch will have the same, except for the soup and the dessert. He'll be talking too much to eat them, anyway." Donna pointed to her drink. "And two more of these. By the way, my date is a very big tipper."

"I would hope so," the waiter said, then scurried off.

"Date?"

Donna gulped her drink, gazed at me for a moment. "Are you having a good time?"

"Oh, yeah, worth every penny."

"Who are you, Micah Frost and what do you want with me?"

"Just a guy with some questions."

"Miles said you were a cross between the Lone Ranger and Sherlock Holmes with a dash of Snidely Whiplash tossed in to round off the corners."

"Miles sure has a way with words."

"Miles likes you, Frost. That makes you automatically suspect."

"He seems to like you, too. Can we be suspect together?"

"How do you know Miles?"

"Miles does a little research for me from time to time."

"How'd you meet him?"

"I met him at a party, if I remember correctly."

Donna snorted. "I believe it was a fairy-bashing party that kicked into gear a couple of hours after the end of the Gay Pride Parade. The way Miles tells it, three skinheads were about to non-

70

FROST

surgically remove his genitalia when you rode in on a white horse and started breaking fingers and noses and spines."

"I've had extensive therapy since then. I can't remember the last time I broke anybody's fingers."

Donna chugged the rest of her drink, emptied it just as the waiter brought the next round. She twirled her index finger about the top of the empty glass, held up two fingers. The waiter nodded, then vanished again. So he stared at me for a moment, then twisted her mouth into a curious smirk.

"Where did you go to art school?"

"I didn't."

"A self-taught reasonably successful artist with a hard-earned reputation for being a thug. Guys like you don't exist."

"Then I'm not picking up this dinner check."

"You draw pictures. You draw the stuff they put in kid's picture books. Mother Goose stuff, but for grownups."

"That's one way to put it."

"And you actually make money at it."

"On occasion."

"Lots of naked ladies. I've seen your work at a couple of exhibitions and if *Playboy* foldouts had been around in the Middle Ages..."

I shrugged. "I paint what I feel."

"And vice-versa, I'll bet."

"I'm flattered you remembered my name."

"I didn't. The Times art critic did. He thinks your stuff is banal, exploitive, and little more than an excuse for masturbation."

"He's right. Interested in posing?"

FROST

"Why is a nice boy like you interested in runaway street kids?"

"Why is a reporter pretending to be a hooker? I'd think that story has been done and done again."

"You first."

I drummed my fingers on the table, started to begin my tale of researching a possible graphic novel, but thought better of it. I gave Donna all of it, bit by bit, the photos, the reunion with my brother, the break-in at my house, Camey's murder, runaway kids, twisted corporate ownership, the perversion catalog decoded by our mutual friend Miles, undocumented millions of dollars and my unrealized tie to this whole damn mess.

Donna ate her steak and most of mine, soup, dessert, another drink and two cups of black coffee. "There are more than six of them," she said. "These kids come and go, they rotate locations, travel from downtown to Capitol Hill to the University District and beyond. Some find a crib, some find a sugar daddy, and some find a needle and die."

"How many?"

"Hard to say. It's hard to track these kids."

"How'd you get on this?"

"This kid walked into the newsroom about three weeks ago. Lived on the streets with his brother. Anyway, he says his brother just up and went, and from what I've been able to determine this kid wasn't the first to just disappear."

"Why are you dressed like a hooker?"

"Easier to watch the nightlife if you look like you belong. How'd you know I wasn't one?"

I spoke to Donna briefly about the concept of kneeling.

FROST

We walked through Belltown and down toward Western, came to rest at the entrance to a newly refurbished warehouse converted to condominiums.

"This girl Camey--were you in love with her?"

"No. I liked her, though."

Donna looked me up and down. "Lucky her."

"Not so much."

"Meet me here tomorrow morning. We'll go talk to some of these kids."

"Do I have to buy you breakfast?"

"I don't eat breakfast."

"Thank goodness."

"I eat brunch, around ten. Be here at nine-thirty."

***

Blondie, Bozo and Dick Dastardly sat on the trunk of my car. The three watched me approach with seeming disinterest. I walked past them, turned, leaned against the car door.

"I think perhaps you're waiting for me."

"You must be Frost," Blondie said.

"You must be a complete idiot."

The trio slid off the trunk and walked toward me. "You've got a big mouth for such a little guy."

"I'm sorry. I hope I didn't upset you."

Blondie bawled a right fist around the base of a tire iron, tapped it against his left palm. He stepped forward, sneered. "We've got a message for you."

FROST

"What's that?"

He snickered. "It's in Morse code."

I shook my head, shoved my left hand toward him and pulled the trigger. The Colt popped once, sounded like a walnut shell caught in a metal vise. Blondie screamed, fell to the ground clutching his shattered kneecap.

Bozo and Dastardly looked at me with a newfound respect. "Gentlemen, take off your pants."

Both grudgingly complied. I ordered them to place the garments on the ground and take two giant steps backward. "You, Blondie--toss your wallet over here, and you two morons, as well. Nice and easy, I've got five shots left."

I unlocked the Dart, backslid into the driver's seat and started her up. Door open, left hand angling the pistol toward the trio, I let it run for a moment, revved the engine, then pulled away from the parking slot. I popped the car out of gear, climbed out of the car and fetched the three wallets and the two pair of pants, then tossed them all into the passenger front floorboard. I reclaimed my seat inside.

"Better get Blondie to a hospital before he bleeds to death," I said. I popped the transmission into Drive and pulled away, left the amateurs in the parking lot.

***

I released the clip from the little .25 Caliber, sat the gun on the coffee table and thumbed the shells out of the metal case. I doubted Blondie and the boys would bother filing a complaint, but a change of weaponry would offer protection against a ballistics

FROST

check. I am licensed to carry and the first step in the event of a complaint would be to impound my handgun.

I carried the Colt into the basement. Another doper hidey-hole tucked behind the fireplace's brick support. I walked behind the chimney and pulled out two of the bricks, releasing a hinge lock. The panel swung open, revealing my private arsenal.

Eight identical Colt .25 automatics clung to the inside wall of the structure. I'd purchased the guns at swap meets and private weapons exhibitions for cash and I knew they were clean. I'd done some very touchy work for a gunsmith some years ago and the man was grateful enough to work over each handgun as I bought them. He checked the mechanisms, squared the sights, cleaned and oiled the insides, carefully calibrated them, re-blued the finish, then carefully doctored the imprinted serial number so that every one of the Colts bore the same manufacturer's identification code. Any ballistic test would show clear because even though the serial number would match my license, the slug would expel from a different weapon.

I chose a Colt at random, pulled it off the holder and replaced it with the weapon I'd used the shatter Blondie's kneecap, then closed the door to the weapon cache.

Back upstairs, I took the three wallets acquired earlier that evening, pulled the cash out of them and tossed them into the same hidden panel that held Pear's purloined address book.

I couldn't help smiling when I counted the wad of cash in my hand. Shooting Blondie and pantsing his partners earned me almost two thousand dollars.

FROST

Chapter Twelve

I picked up Donna Trent at nine-thirty Saturday morning, drove to Virginia Avenue and parked in the same lot as the night before. Blondie and the boys were long gone and this particular lot at the corner of Third Avenue has the least expensive downtown parking rate of any centrally located lot I've found.

We walked to Pike's Market and Donna led me to a counter seat at Three Girls' Bakery. She ordered for both of us, cinnamon rolls half the size of a man's shoebox and two large black coffees.

"My treat," she said.

"I most certainly hope so."

"Tell me," Donna said, digging into her cinnamon roll with a plastic spoon-and-fork combo, "how'd you get into the Private Investigator business?"

"I'm not in the business. I sometimes do favors for people I like who have no other options. I'm kind of a *thug-of-last-resort.*"

Donna watched me for a moment, then licked her lips and shoveled in another chunk of gooey pastry. "You have a license."

I sipped the coffee, tapped a finger against the rim of the cup. "The license is a convenience. Somewhere along the way I managed to pick up a certain specialized problem solving ability. My vocation allows more flexibility in scheduling the time to deal with shall we say occasionally cumbersome matters."

"You should be in politics, Mr. Frost."

"This is too often close enough."

FROST

"Y'know, Sam Rollins tells me you may be the best there is at what you do. Greg Ahmann tells me you're an incompetent buttbrain. Miles tells me you're Mr. Terrific."

"Two out of three, as they say. Who else did you check with?"

"I ran you through the morgue at the paper. Interesting reading. You make a lot of people angry, Mr. Frost."

"Genuine lack of social skills."

"Offhand, I'd say it was a genuine inability to tolerate assholes."

"Is that good, bad or indifferent?"

Donna pushed away her empty paper plate. "Are you going to eat that?"

I shoved my untouched cinnamon roll toward her.

"Thanks. Here's the thing: I don't know what your real story is, Micah, and that scares me. I'm about to bring you into my story and I don't know how you'll react. The things I hear do not make me confident you'll be much interested in finding some kind of middle ground to negotiate from. And I'm nosey. Most reporters are."

"What is it you want, Miss Trent?"

Donna took another bite and swallowed. "I have every confidence you'll close this thing up, eventually, the question is how many bodies you'll run through to do it. Bodies are going to fall, including a number of very powerful people if what you told me last night is true, and I believe it is. I want to work with you on this. I want first crack at everything you come across."

"How do you propose this partnership operate?"

"I know our agendas are different, but it seems to me that the same highway might take us to both our destinations. If these missing kids are tied to this Stone guy I want to make sure he gets the blame for it. In return, you'll get everything I've got and everything I get. I'm bound to have some sources you don't."

"Fair enough, but when you write this up you leave me out of the story."

Donna twisted her features into an annoyed grimace. "I don't know that I can do that."

"Then I'm certain I won't discover anything that would be of interest to you."

Donna looked at me for a long moment, wide-eyed and probing. Finally, she laughed a bit. "Okay, Cranston, I'll leave you out of the piece."

Donna thrust an open hand at me and I wrapped my fingers around it and shook.

"Thanks, Margo."

***

The place had at one time been a reasonably elegant hotel, but time slipped by and need slipped away, leaving only vague memories wrapped in chipped stone.

Donna and I stepped through a battered alley doorway and into a darkened hallway. Sunlight shone through slits of rotted boards nailed over unglassed windows and dust floated freely inside those narrow golden beams. The stench of urine and excrement coated the walls and the floors. I wondered momentarily which was worse, to breathe through my nose and smell it or to breathe through my mouth and coat my teeth.

Donna stormed boldly up a creaking stairwell. I followed, wondering at the circumstances that would make this living arrangement preferable to tolerating the idiosyncrasies of a parent, then remembered my own childhood and answered my question.

Like the guy said in that movie, *we're all alone out there, folks, and tomorrow we're going out there again.*

Donna turned right at the top of the stairs, walked to the first door and tapped lightly. "Matthew, it's Donna Trent."

The boy pulled open the door, looked sullenly at Donna. "Who's he?"

"He's okay, Matthew. He's a friend."

"Call me Micah."

The boy turned and walked back inside the room. A tattered backpack sat in a corner, a couple of grungy blankets spread across a ruined wooden floor. Matthew leaned against a wall, crossed his arms.

"Heard anything from your brother, Matthew?" Donna motioned me inside and closed the door.

"Paul ain't comin' back."

"Why do you say that?"

"He's been gone too long. He's either split for good or he's dead."

"Which do you think?" I asked.

Matthew shrugged. His eyes moistened and he fought to blink away tears. "He'd come for me if he could. I think he's dead."

The boy struggled to be cold and tough. He'd been on the streets long enough to know the drill, but the lines didn't work for him.

"How old are you, Matthew? Nine, ten?"

FROST

Tears welled in the corners of the boy's eyes, rolled through the grime on his cheeks. "Old enough."

"Matthew, you let me know if you hear from Paul, okay?" The boy nodded. Donna turned toward the door and looked at me. "Let's go."

I ignored her, walked toward the boy. "We're going to go get some lunch. Would you like to come?"

Matthew looked at me uncertainly. "I don't--"

"My treat."

The boy looked at Donna, then back at me. "I can't go."

"You can go."

"Micah--"

"Quiet, Donna. Matt--can I call you Matt?--your brother is gone. You said it yourself, if he could come for you he would have. This is not a good place for you. You are not safe here. When's the last time you had a hot meal, Matt?"

"I eat."

"You scavenge. You nibble. Mostly, you hide because you're small and you've seen what happens to small on these streets."

Matt's lips began to quiver.

"Matt, I can't make everything better, but I can make some of it better, and I can do that right now. Get your things."

"My brother--"

"If he can be found, I'll find him. I promise."

"You're gonna send me back--"

"I'm not going to send you anywhere. I'm not going to turn you over to juvie and I won't let anyone else turn you in, either. And nobody will try to send you back home unless you decide

FROST

that's the best thing for you." I reached toward him. "Would you like to join us for lunch?"

Matt bit his lower lip, fought to control his heaving concave chest. "Okay," he murmured, reached out and grasped my hand.

"Well, I'll be dipped," Donna said.

The boy slipped his hand from mine, slid to his backpack. He picked up the bag and walked back to me, took my hand again. "What's for lunch?"

I gazed into his dirty brown face and grinned. "What would you like, Matt?"

We found a McDonald's on the waterfront and Matt inhaled three quarter pounders, two orders of fries and a chocolate milkshake. I led him into the men's room after the meal and tried to clean him up a bit, but the tools I found to work with were woefully inadequate.

Donna, Matt and I ascended the hill climb behind Pike's Market and found our way to Fifth Avenue and the downtown Nordstrom.

"Hello, Miss Trent." Helen Myerson's name tag identified her as a Personal Shopping Specialist.

"Good morning, Helen. These two gentlemen--" she waved a hand at Matt and me "--are very dear friends of mine. Matthew, he's the good-looking one, has come to the end of a long, frightening journey in which most everything he owns has been lost to him."

Helen Myerson twisted her pert, painted features into an appropriate grimace of sympathy. "Oohhhhh," she purred.

"He's going to need everything, I'm afraid, pants, shirts, a couple of sweaters, some good leather shoes, and some kind of dress jacket. Underwear and socks, of course."

FROST

Matt looked up at me, terrified.

"And sneakers," I said, winking at the boy. "Boots, too. Jeans, a couple of pairs. And a lightweight Autumn jacket, something without the name of a sports team on it."

"And, I think, a new backpack," Donna added.

"Very good," Helen Myerson informed us. "We have a shower facility upstairs. Normally, it's reserved for employees who want to work out during the lunch hour, but we might make an exception in this case if the gentleman is so inclined."

Donna grinned at the boy. "Are you so inclined, Matthew?"

The boy shoved his hands into the pockets of his ratty denim jacket. "I can take a shower, I s'pose."

We all climbed into the elevator and rode to the top floor of the Nordstrom building. Helen Myerson led us beyond the Sales Floor through two heavy swinging doors marked *STAFF ONLY*, past a stock area and into an Employee Lounge. She checked the stall, assured herself the shower was indeed unoccupied, then disappeared. She returned momentarily with small samples of soap, shampoo and two very large plush blue bath towels.

"Is she going to make sure he washes behind his ears?" I asked.

Donna nudged me in the ribs with her elbow. "That's your job, Mr. Frost."

"Me?"

"Yeah, you, tough guy."

"Don't tell anybody about this. I have an image to maintain."

"Fingers and noses and spines, oh my!"

We spent the next couple of hours helping Matt feel like a child. I toweled his hair dry, wrapped him in a dry towel and

FROST

carted him downstairs to Young Men's Wear. We bought him clothing, got him dressed. Donna found him a black diving watch and I picked out man's leather wallet and tucked a couple of ten dollar bills inside when he wasn't looking.

Donna hauled us into Zanadu Comics and helped Matt pick out half-a-dozen comic books.

By now we were all hungry again, so we hopped on a bus toward Belltown and collapsed inside the Five Points Grill. We all ordered fried chicken, and when Matt said he was thirsty I offered him coffee.

"Black," Matt said, "just like yours."

"You can't feed him coffee," Donna said.

"He's too young for beer."

"Not if it's really good beer," Matt said. We both glared at the boy and he giggled aloud, a kid once again.

***

"What are you going to do with me?"

The three of us sat in Donna's condominium, sipping on coffee and Dr. Pepper.

"I think you'll stay with me for a while," Donna said. "Micah's place is just a little too interesting for a boy your age. If anyone asks, you're my nephew."

Matt carefully sat the plastic soft-drink bottle on the hand-painted coaster in front of him. "How long is awhile?"

I told him he wouldn't be going back on the street again, ever.

"I can't go home."

"I know."

FROST

"Social workers send me home. They did, twice."

"No social workers, Matt. If you're scared to go home, you don't have to go there." Matt looked up at me and I could see the desperation creep into his eyes. "I promise."

Donna tucked him into her guest room, waited for him to fall asleep. She slipped out of the room, came and sat beside me. "He may have to be returned to his parents, Micah. You might not have a choice."

"There's always a choice, Donna."

"Micah--"

"You didn't see him in the shower. The boy is covered with scars, and unless I miss my guess they're from cigarette burns. Do you have any idea how long you have to hold a lit cigarette against human flesh to cause permanent scarring?"

Donna winced.

"Matt won't go back to his parents. Period."

"Because you promised."

"I promised."

"Do you always keep your promises?"

"No, but I try to keep the important ones."

"You could find yourself in a hell of a lot of trouble, Mr. Frost."

"That's actually the tagline on my business card."

FROST

Chapter Thirteen

I parked the Dart, grabbed my camera and my coffee and crossed Alki Avenue to the beach. I settled atop a concrete piling and gazed at the Halleck monstrosity above me.

Lights were on at all four levels, curtains opened to exploit the view of the Sound. I punched the telephoto button on the camera and looked at the viewer. Blondie hobbled past the third floor picture window, a crutch shoved under his right armpit. The two teenaged girls I'd seen Thursday stood sipping what appeared to be some kind of cola. I snapped a shot of both young faces, scanned the room, but found no one else to immortalize.

I focused on the top floor. The angle from the beach made it difficult to see much detail until I discovered the large mirror mounted above the fireplace mantle. I refocused the lens on the mirror and managed to snap two clean reversed images of another kid and a middle-aged man in jeans and a sport coat.

The second floor was apparently the entry level. Dick Dastardly leaned against the wall beside the front door. I watched him open it twice, and admit new guests. I dutifully recorded them for posterity.

The first floor remained lit, but empty, for the next hour. Bozo wandered in, picked up a cardboard box and carried it upstairs. I clicked his image, as well.

Three more guests arrived. I didn't recognize any of them, took their pictures anyway. I also managed to record three more kids.

FROST

The curtains closed shortly after the arrival of the last three guests. I slurped the last dregs of the cold coffee and zipped back to my car.

I pulled away from the beach, pointed the Dart toward Queen Anne. The West Lee house was dark and silent, the red BMW nowhere in sight. The windows were closed and locked now, so I shoved a gloved hand through a pane of bedroom window glass and climbed inside.

I removed the SDHC Card from the camera mounted above the bed and dropped it into a small plastic sleeve, then inside the leather satchel I'd slung over my shoulder.

I plundered the drawers in the dresser and the clothes chest, found three more film cards and tossed them into my bag. I made a run through the rest of the house, found nothing I thought might be useful until I approached a computer desk in the upstairs bedroom. A dozen boxes of empty flashdrives sat on a shelf by the laptop alongside a black tooled leather case. The case held six flashdrives, each simply slugged *STONE*. I dropped the drives into the satchel and slipped back downstairs.

Tradition maintained is a wonderful thing, so on my way out I opened the refrigerator and pilfered two more bottles of Henry's.

***

I left the flashdrives with Miles. He was on his way out, but promised to attack them the next morning. I carried the film cards home with me.

I slid the first card into my laptop and Camey flashed onscreen, naked and alone. It took a moment to get used to the

FROST

dizzying angle. Camey caressed herself, hands gently stroking her nipples, rubbing the insides of her thighs.

A dull fullness settled into my chest. I double-clicked on the fast-forward icon, scanned the rest of the card and then removed it.

The second card featured Dolly Michelle and Pear. Fingers pulled every juncture, tongues probed every orifice. Pear gracelessly crammed himself into every conceivable cavity of Michelle's body, including a few I'd never even considered.

The third card flashed Michelle again, wrists and ankles strapped to the corners of the bed with leather straps. Another wide slash of cowhide stretched across the lower half of her face. Her eyes bulged in terror. Pear squatted between her ankles, chewing at the apex of Michelle's thighs. He pulled away and blood oozed across the snow white sheets. Pear slapped the girl's breasts, grabbed a nipple and pinched, then twisted. Michelle struggled against her bonds, but the straps held fast. I punched the fast-forward icon, verified Pear and Michelle as the only participants in this seedy little drama, then pulled the card from the laptop slot.

The fourth card was mercifully empty.

I dropped all four cards into an envelope, tucked it inside a hidden alcove above the laundry chute and washed my hands.

**

I thought it was the doorbell at first. I stumbled through slumber's fog, found the clock on the nightstand and read two-oh-five, actually mumbled it aloud. The phone rang again, the landline, not my cellphone. I pulled the receiver to my ear.

87

FROST

"I believe you have something that belongs to me," a voice said. I didn't recognize it.

"What would that be?"

"Would you prefer to deliver it or shall I have it picked up?"

Glass shattered. Muffled footsteps pounded the hardwood floor in my living room. I grabbed the Colt and tumbled to the floor, crammed myself into the small space between the end of the wooden dresser and the wall.

Bozo and Dick Dastardly erupted through the bedroom door. Bozo emptied both barrels of a sawed-off shotgun into the mattress while Dastardly sprayed an Uzi into the hand-carved headboard.

I bounced to my knees, slammed my right leg into the side of the wooden dresser. I felt my leg go numb, tried to ignore it. I shoved the Colt in front of me and pointed, pulled the trigger.

Dastardly dropped the Uzi and clutched at his throat. He tried to scream, able only to bleat a liquefied gurgle.

Bozo frantically leapt toward the fallen Uzi. He grasped the shotgun with his left hand, pulled it up over his shoulder as if to throw it at me.

I shot him twice in the gut.

I turned on the light switch and walked to where the boys were. Dastardly's glassed eyes stared lifelessly at the ceiling. Bozo clutched his blood-smeared abdomen, his lips chattered, his tongue pulled at the air. A thin trail of blood seeped from the corner of his mouth. I squatted near him. He tried to spit at me, couldn't find the energy. I grabbed his chin with my fingers, pressed hard. "Did you do Camey Horne?"

FROST

Bozo chortled, red bubbles sliding down his chin and onto my hand. "We all three did her," he wheezed. "Right after we nailed her to the counter."

It took a moment for his statement to sink in.

"She wasn't that good."

I pushed the Colt's short barrel into Bozo's left eyeball and pulled the trigger.

FROST

Chapter Fourteen

Sam Rollins kicked at a piece of shattered stained glass. "Your landlord's gonna love this."

"I won't tell him."

Sam nodded at the KOMO News Van parked across the street. "You probably won't have to."

"I always wanted to be a celebrity."

"That snazzy dressing gown isn't going to play well on the morning broadcast."

I glanced down at the well-worn burgundy terry cloth bathrobe wrapped around my shoulders. "Can't let stardom go to my head."

"You wouldn't happen to know those two guys, would you buddy?"

"Would you like a beer?"

"Micah--"

"No."

"And of course you have no idea why they'd come flying through your front window in the middle of the night."

"Certainly not." I turned up the collar of the bathrobe. "Think you could talk your lab boys into letting me get some clothes? It's kind of drafty in here."

Sam glared at me, turned and stormed toward my bedroom. He returned a moment later with jeans, a long sleeve cotton sweater and a pair of Docksiders.

"No socks? No underwear?"

Sam threw the clothes at me. "You've survived worse."

FROST

I pulled open the robe, dropped it on the floor. I stepped into the jeans and the Docksiders and jerked the orange sweater over my head. Sam watched in silence. I knew what he wanted, but I also knew he was a good by-the-book cop and he'd do the job he was paid to do if he had the evidence to point him in the right direction.

He'd get no direction from me. Pear was mine, and I wasn't ready to tie Bozo and Dick Dastardly to my fraternal twin so someone else could dig around and pull him in.

"This used to be a drug house, Sam."

"So?'

"Manufacturing and wholesale, actually. Grew the stuff right in the basement, harvested the leaves, dried them out and chopped them up. I understand they sold in bulk."

Sam cocked one eyebrow. "Pot's legal in Washington, Micah."

I shook a finger in the air. "Not in bulk and not without a permit. I think perhaps these two meant to rob and plunder a dealer, maybe somebody who supplies to other states that are not so, what's the word, progressive? Only maybe they didn't know the doper doesn't live here anymore."

"How long have you lived here?"

"Almost a year."

"Must have been some fairly stupid young gentlemen. All they had to do was read the name on the mailbox."

"I blame the public education system."

"I mean, they certainly wouldn't have knowingly come blazing in here in the middle of the night with the idea of taking you out?"

I smiled. "Sam, nobody is that stupid."

FROST

The coroner's people hauled the corpses away forty-five minutes later and the lab boys tagged along behind them. Soon, everyone had gone but Sam and me. Alone, he asked if the offer of a beer still held, and I fetched the two pilfered Henry's from the refrigerator.

"It's amazing how in a desperate struggle your gun could go off at just the right angle and at the precise moment you plunged it behind that guy's eyeliner."

"Isn't it, though? I'd like to credit my reflexes, but just not as young and fast as I used to be. Must've been, I don't know, Karma maybe."

"Karma. You're lucky I was here. Somebody not as familiar with your sense of character might have wondered if maybe you'd gotten the drop on the fella and made a conscious choice to blow out the back of his skull."

"It wouldn't make a difference, Sam. Two jackasses break into my home in the middle of the night pulling triggers and I defended myself. At least that's what my attorney would say and we both know a jury would buy it."

"So you're changing your story?"

"Of course not. I would never voluntarily ruin bedroom carpet in such an irresponsible manner."

***

The stained glass picture window lay in several large and a great many small pieces on my living room hardwood floor. I hoped the forecasted rain would hold off until after I'd gotten someone out to at least board up the opening. The bedroom door was splintered and the plastered wall boasted a couple of fist-sized

FROST

holes. The pearl grey carpet blotched crimson in several spots. At least Crickett hadn't been here to get caught in the crossfire.

I changed my clothes, slipped into socks and cowboy boots and exchanged the light cotton sweater for a heavier black turtleneck.

The lab boys packed my gun and took it with them. The arsenal in the basement did me no good thanks to the precautionary doctoring of the serial numbers on each weapon, so I walked to the Dodge, popped the trunk and retrieved the Ruger .357 I kept clipped behind the tire jack. A tooled leather shoulder holster hung inside the guest room closet and I shoved the cannon into it, pulled on the harness and adjusted the straps. I preferred the Colt: it was less obtrusive, quicker to access, easier to handle and didn't require wearing a jacket. At least the Autumn weather made the bundling more comfortable.

I grabbed a navy windbreaker from my closet. I wouldn't need to cover the Ruger where I was going, but I wasn't about to take it off and I'd probably want to stop for breakfast.

FROST

Chapter Fifteen

The Halleck house was dark and quiet. One small light burned in the corner window of the second level. I pulled the Dodge past the house, rounded the corner and parked.

I peeked into the window as I climbed the concrete steps alongside the house. Blondie, also known as David Welsh according to the motorcycle registration, snoozed at the dining table. A small color television flickered from the kitchen counter.

I knocked at the door and stepped back so I could see Blondie's reaction through the window. He barely stirred. I edged up to the open window and called his name.

"Whoosis?"

"Come on, Dave, let us in."

"Y'Okay."

Blondie yawned, pushed himself away from the table. He grabbed an aluminum crutch, shoved it under his arm and hobbled toward the door. I pulled the Ruger out of its harness and put my shoulder just above the ornate doorknob. The bolt lock clicked and the doorknob turned against the back of my left hand. I shoved off of my heels and bashed Blondie with the door, knocked him on his butt. He scrambled to retrieve the crutch, but I shoved the toe of my pointed cowboy boot into his crotch.

Blondie crammed both arms between his thighs and howled. I turned and closed the door, propped my knee against his own bandaged leg and shoved the Ruger's barrel into his nostril.

"Your friends are dead."

FROST

Blondie rolled his eyes. "What friends?" he wheezed.

"The two junior idiots who hauled you in for legwork, buttbrain."

He took a short breath. "I'll miss them."

"I might not get the opportunity."

"You're hurting my leg," he said through clenched teeth.

"Good." I shifted my weight and pressed my knee into the bandage. Blondie screamed and I backed off, allowed him to catch his breath.

"You're going to kill me," he said, finally.

"I'm giving it some serious thought." I cocked the Ruger's hammer.

Blondie closed his eyes. "P-pp-ppplease..."

"Tell me about Stone."

"He paid me two grand to rough you up. I took Steve and Jeremy, paid them five-hundred each. You took the money."

"What did Stone pay you for tonight?"

"Didn't pay me anything. He didn't know."

I slammed all my weight into Blondie's damaged kneecap. He found a scream, lost it when I cuffed him with the pistol. A thin trail of blood oozed from his temple. I stood up, looked at the pile of excrement clumped on the floor in front of me and jammed my boot heel into his ribs. Something audibly cracked, and I kicked again, twice.

I checked the light fixtures in the living room. Sure enough, two hidden video lenses. I removed the cards from the devices, then headed up the stairs. Two bedrooms were unoccupied. I found cameras in both of them and removed those cards as well.

FROST

I slipped up the final flight and entered the first bedroom on the left and turned on the light switch. The two teenaged girls I'd seen earlier sat up in the bed. Both were naked and made no effort to cover themselves.

"I thought everyone left," one of the girls said.

"They did," I answered. "Are you two here because you want to be?"

"What do you care?" Sunken eyes flared with hatred beneath dirty blonde hair. The girl threw back the covers and lifted her legs into the air, parted them at the ankles. "What's your pleasure, mister?"

I walked to the light fixture in the center of the room, jerked the camera out of it and removed the card. "You don't want to be here, you don't have to be."

"Right."

"You can leave, right now."

The two girls looked at each other. "And go where?"

"Does it matter? It can't be any worse than this."

"Are you going to fuck me?"

"No."

The girl lowered herself into the bed and pulled the sheet over herself. "Turn the light off on your way out."

The other girl gave me the once-over. I saw the struggle beneath her eyes, watched her hands clench and unclench. "Get some clothes on."

The girl hesitated, then grabbed a pair of jeans and a tee-shirt and pulled them on under a denim jacket.

"Anything here you have to have?"

"Just me," she said.

"Could you carry these for me?"

FROST

"Sure." She took the plastic bag of SDHC cards I'd collected, twisted the bag closed. "Where to?"

"Out of here."

We scrambled down the stairs, stopped at the landing. Blondie piled in a heap against the far wall. The girl tried not to look at him, stepped away as if he might at any moment snap back to life and clutch at her.

She followed me to the Dart. I unlocked the car door and helped her inside. We drove into the hazy light of sunrise, away from the four-storied cage where I'd found her.

"My name is Micah."

"Serena."

"Very pretty name. I'm proud to know you, Serena."

"Are you a cop?"

"Not even close."

Serena folded her hands across her lap and looked straight ahead.

"Do you mind if I ask how old you are?"

"How old do you want me to be?"

"As old as you are."

"Sixteen."

"How'd you hook up with David Welsh?"

Serena twisted in her seat. "What are you going to with me?"

"What do you want me to do with you? Is there someplace I can take you?"

"No. I guess I'm just yours."

"Serena, what can you tell me about David Welsh?"

"Then you'll let me go?"

FROST

I pulled the car over to the curb. "The door isn't locked. You can go now if you want to, but I really need some help."

Serena grabbed the door handle and pulled it. The door swung open and she twisted in the seat. I didn't move. She waited, then swung a leg outside the car, waited to see if I'd try to grab her, seemed to relax a bit when I didn't. Finally, she twisted back inside the car and closed the door. "Marjorie," she said.

"Marjorie?"

"The other girl in the room. I met her on the street. She said she had some friends we could stay with, brought me over here on the bus. David got us inside, fed me, and then told me the place was a whore house." She clenched her fists. "I told him I wasn't interested, but he wouldn't let me leave. Him and Steve and Jeremy dragged me upstairs and--" Tears ran down her cheeks.

"And then?"

"They wouldn't let me leave. The three of them took turns at me for a few days, they'd--*take me*, then they'd beat me up. Wouldn't let me leave, wouldn't feed me. I gave up after about a week." Serena slumped down into the seat, leaned against the car door. "I didn't have anywhere to go, anyway."

We drove in silence. I pulled onto the West Seattle Bridge, found Highway 99 and headed toward Ballard. Hattie's Hat served a pretty good breakfast and eating would give me some time to think. I hadn't planned on a sixteen-year-old female houseguest, especially when the house was now literally a shambled mess.

I herded Serena toward a back booth and ordered steak and eggs for both of us. She picked at her food and didn't talk much. I tried this and this, but the girl wouldn't open up. I looked into her dull green eyes and found nothing but hopelessness.

"Serena, if you could have anything in the world, what would that be?"

"I don't know. A real life with a future, maybe."

"And what is that? What does that mean to you?"

"Some kind of career, maybe. College. A place of my own, so I don't have to depend on anybody else."

"What kind of career?"

"What's the difference? It isn't going to happen."

"It could."

"Oh, right."

"How long ago did you leave home?"

"Three months."

"Do you want to go back?"

Serena's eyes flashed. "I'm not going back."

"You don't have to."

"Damned right I don't."

I grinned at the girl. "Serena, I think you're going to do just fine."

"Yeah, I've got the world by the balls."

"Suppose for a moment that I could help you get what you want--a decent place to live, education, a car, enough money to be self-sufficient until you can do it on your own. Would you be willing to help me get the people who did this to you? Not just David, but the people he works for, too."

Serena gazed thoughtfully at me "What would I have to do?"

"Pretend you're pregnant."

FROST

***

I called Miles after Serena and I finished talking. He opened his apartment door wearing a yellow silk kimono emblazoned with red dragons and orange flames. Serena looked at him warily, but he turned on his considerable charm and soon had the girl laughing out loud.

I pulled Miles aside, gave him a chunk of the money I'd earned bashing Blondie and the boys, and told him to get the girl cleaned up and take her shopping. "Let her make the clothing choices."

"Don't you trust my taste?"

"No."

"Bitch."

"And for the record, I don't want to find any part of her newly pierced or tattooed."

"Anything else, Dad?"

"Have her home by midnight."

***

I called Donna Trent after I parked outside her condo. Matt opened the door, grinned up at me. "Hey, Micah."

"Hey yourself, Matt." I stepped inside and closed the door.

Donna sat on the sofa swiping at a notebook screen. I sat down beside her, looked over her shoulder into a series of jpegs apparently from the flashdrive I'd acquired at Pear's house.

"Where did you get that?"

"I have my sources."

"Does he wear lipstick and eyeliner?"

100

FROST

"That's offensive."

"It's only offensive when he overdoes it."

"Miles does work for me from time to time. He knows we're working on this together. Have you taken a close look at this thing?"

"I scanned it."

"You've got some very powerful people in some very compromising positions."

"Sounds like an ad campaign for a new cologne."

Donna got up and walked across the living room into the kitchen. She reappeared in a few moments with two mugs of steaming coffee and sat one in front of me.

"You've got two well-known rock stars," I said, nodding at the screen. "A best-selling novelist, the Chairman of one of Puget Sound's biggest employers, a major movie star, and a genuine United States Congressman, all of them with homes in the greater Seattle area."

"You scan very well."

"Something tells me everybody on that drive is well-off, which means they can afford good legal representation. Not that it matters, we can't tie this to any of them."

Donna scowled. "What do you mean?"

"Computer images are too easily manipulated, bodies are scanned and resized, features reformed or replaced. Any second year computer student, or art student for that matter, should be able to do an exceptional job of it."

"You think these are phony?"

"No, I think they're real. These people wouldn't be paying money to Stone if they weren't real. My guess is they don't know what he might have in the way of confirmation, and anyway the publicity would kill all of their careers."

Donna sipped her coffee. "What now, Cranston?"

"Did you notice the deposit dates on the ledger file?"

"No."

"They're all made on the thirteen day of the month, first month of the quarter. Not a single variation."

"Okay."

"Stone has them set up with what I'll bet is an automatic Electronic Funds Transfer."

"An EFT confirmation plus these images with deposit details--"

"--becomes much more difficult to defend. Miles can't figure institution codes for the deposit accounts--"

"--but maybe I can backtrack the originating accounts."

"Can you?"

"I can try. What are you going to do?"

"Who in this crowd of perverts do you think would be the most damaged by public revelation of his extracurricular activities?"

"Wainwright."

"Senator Jonathan. I'm going to send him a congratulatory greeting card."

"Why?"

"He's about to become a father."

FROST

Chapter Sixteen

"Jonathan Wainwright?"

"You're in a hell of a lot of trouble, Mr. Frost."

"It would appear that you are the one in a hell of a lot of trouble, Senator."

We sat at a corner table in the Pike's Place Bar & Grill. I sipped on a Bloody Mary, Wainwright tongued a Vodka Martini. He pulled the speared onion out of the glass, slurped the whole mess into his mouth, spat the bare toothpick back into the tumbler.

"You say I'm about to become a father."

"So I'm told."

"Who is the mother, Mr. Frost?" Wainwright motioned to a waiter, swirled his finger around the top of his glass.

"A sixteen-year-old girl named Serena."

"Serena who?"

"Nice try."

"This is preposterous."

I reached inside my jacket pocket and produced a four-by-five inch manila envelope. Miles had lifted the Senator's portrait from the porn catalog and, using some program or other on his computer, replaced Wainwright's youthful partner's face with Serena's.

I was betting Wainwright wouldn't remember each and every underage girl he'd rented from Pear.

FROST

Wainwright glanced at the prints and slid them back into the envelope, then tucked the packet into an inside pocket. "You don't mind if I keep these?"

"Not at all. I've got the original video."

"I intend to put these into the hands of an expert who'll certify that in his opinion these are superimposed forgeries."

"Do you also have an expert who will certify that the DNA test results we'll petition the court for after the child is born is also a forgery?"

"DNA test?"

"Amazing procedure. The old blood test used to determine paternity could be argued with, but this test charts your genetic material and compares it to the child's. I understand it's ninety-nine point ninety-eight percent accurate."

"Okay," Wainwright snarled, "you've got a pregnant girl. Get rid of it."

"Stone invests an awful lot in these kids, Senator. For instance, this young lady has been held against her will in a room since, well, you know. Stone had her tucked away to see if your union might bear fruit. It's a gamble, generally doesn't work out, but every once in a while--"

"Where is she?"

"Safe."

"Why'd Stone send you? Why didn't he come himself?"

"I don't know. I don't work for him."

Wainwright slammed his fist against the table. The room skidded into silence. He looked around the room, smiled. "Clumsy of me," he said, too loudly. He waited for the noise level to rebuild, then said, "I thought--"

FROST

"You thought your arrangement with Stone was a secure one."

The Senator stared at me for a long moment.

"Here's what we've got, Wainwright--"

"*Senator* Wainwright."

"Not for long."

Wainwright shifted in his chair. "How much?"

"I beg your pardon?"

"What do you want?"

"I don't want anything."

"Nothing at all?"

"Well, there is one little thing."

Wainwright snorted. "And what might that be?

"I want you to think about who else might be able to access this stuff. I mean, this little video could find its way onto the Internet, get picked up by a couple of celebrity porn sites. You could be world famous in literally just a couple of hours."

The color slowly drained from Wainwright's face.

"And if we loop that very short tape, you could even wind up as some other perverts screensaver."

"You son-of-a---"

I waggled my finger in the air.

Wainwright wrapped his finger around a spoon. His knuckles turned white and I saw the thing bend in his grasp. "What is it you want?"

"I want you to pay the check. Leave the waitress a nice tip." I pushed myself away from the table and walked out of the restaurant.

***

FROST

Two of them leaned against the Dart. These two were professionals, slender, muscular, dressed to blend into a crowd. I slid my hand under my jacket, reached to the small of my pack to palm the Colt, then remembered the Colt wasn't there.

I couldn't figure out a way to palm the Ruger in broad daylight without causing a panic, so I didn't. I walked to within ten feet of them and stopped. "Would you gentlemen kindly peel your asses off of my car?"

The one on the left pulled deeply on his cigarette, let the smoke drift out of his nostrils. He twisted the cigarette between his thumb and index finger, then ground it out on the Dodge's green vinyl top. "You call this a car?"

"It's a good car, really," the other thug said. "Automatic, power steering, power brakes. He could drive this thing with two broken arms and one broken leg."

I folded my arms across my chest, slipped my right hand inside my jacket and gripped the butt of the Ruger.

The first thug smiled, white, tiny, even teeth shining through a trim blonde beard. "Assuming the thing doesn't explode when he turns the key in the ignition."

"If he was smart, he'd climb into this beater and explore the climate in some other part of the world, say Mexico or maybe Peru."

"Australia would be good for him. Out of sight, out of mind, out of touch." He paused. "Still alive."

"I couldn't go," I said.

"Why not?"

"I'd miss the charm and warmth you boys bring to this locale."

FROST

The beard pushed at the nosepiece of his sunglasses. "Do yourself a favor, Frost. Walk away. Pack up and get lost."

"All of my stuff won't fit in the car."

"Give some of it away."

"I can't. I like all of it."

"Goodbye, Frost. Next time this won't be a chat."

"Great. I'll bring the bean dip."

I waited for the two of them to reach the edge of the lot, then walked around to the front of the Dart and popped the hood. I didn't find anything I didn't recognize. I took a quick peek under the backend, found exactly what I'd driven in with.

I slipped the key into the ignition, took a deep breath and turned the key. The car fired right up, roared to life and settled into a medium idle.

I pulled the gearshift toward me, dropped it into Reverse and backed into the drive-through lane. I tried to shift into Drive, but the gearshift lever slid over Neutral, then Second, and wouldn't catch. I shoved the lever upward, heard a small pop, a sound not unlike the cork blowing out of a bottle of cheap champagne.

A thin trail of smoke seeped from underneath the dashboard into the car. I smelled burning, snatched the keys and scrambled out of the car.

The explosion tossed me several feet into the air. I landed hard onto the concrete, felt the air push out of my lungs, felt conscious thought evaporate.

FROST

Chapter Seventeen

Miles floated in front of me, turquoise wings fluttering about my head and shoulders. White silk draped across his body. He smelled of lemon wind and rose cologne, and I reached for him, saw my hands pass through his body, clutch at air and suddenly I was falling, dropping away into an abyss, light flashing on and off and on and off, glare and darkness, glimmer and glum, cold wind whooshing through my hair, stinging my eyes, bouncing with the force of a gloved fist cramming into me over and over and over and over and over and over and over and over...

"Micah!"

I tried to focus on the voice, reach toward it.

"Micah!"

I knew the sound and the timbre, couldn't quite place the sound into an owner's mouth.

"Micah!"

I fought the staples that held my eyes shut, ripped at the steel pins, pulled them away from the sockets.

Miles sat next to the bed. He leaned into me, looked into my face as if it were a page of newly discovered erotic fiction.

"I hurt," I said.

"I'm not surprised. Miles reached across me and pressed a red signal button mounted on the opposite bed guard. A voice answered, and Miles informed it I was awake. "Get Dr. Bierman," he said.

FROST

Bierman came into the room a few minutes later. He wiped wire spectacles on the hem of his lab coat, asked me my name, my age, my date of birth, my address.

I asked him his shoe size.

Bierman smiled and shined a penlight into my eyeballs, first the right, then the left, then the right again. I asked if I could keep the penlight, couldn't remember why I'd want it, thanked Bierman when he folded it into my hand.

"You've got a dandy concussion," the doctor told me.

"Dandy."

"Surprisingly, there doesn't seem to be a great deal of other physical damage, just some scraped skin and a lot of bruising. You're very fortunate, Micah. Do you feel numb at all?"

I shook my head. "As a matter of fact, I hurt like hell."

"Good," Bierman said, too cheerfully. "That tells me there's probably no nerve damage."

"Dandy."

Miles slapped at my wrist.

"How long have I been out?"

"Two days," Miles said.

I bolted upright. The room swirled, nausea oozed into me. I eased myself back down.

"You've got a nasty tear at the base of your skull," Bierman said. "Jumping around probably isn't the best idea."

I touched the bandage on the back of my head. "How much hair did you take off?"

"Very little. We put the bulk of it into a ponytail and shaved underneath. When the bandage comes off it probably won't even show."

"Dandy."

FROST

Bierman muttered something about checking in later, told me I could eat whenever I wanted and that he'd be back in the morning.

"Hungry?" Miles asked after the doctor left.

"No. What time is it?"

Miles glanced at his watch. "Eleven thirty-five Tuesday night."

"How's my car?"

"You no longer have a car. You have a hunk of green twisted metal fused with flecks of rubber and vinyl."

"Dandy." I clicked the penlight on and off several times. "How long have you been sitting here?"

"Since about eight this evening. Chelsea was here before me, Donna before her. We've been clocking in and out like a regular task force."

"Thanks, Miles."

"Don't go all soft on me, Frost. Anyway, you'd do it for me."

"Like hell I would."

"Sam Rollins was in a couple of times. He told me to call him if and when you came around."

"Better give him a yell."

Miles pulled a business card from inside his billfold, reached for his cellphone and punched in the number.

***

I dozed. I awoke to find Sam Rollins sitting alone in my room.

"How are you doing?"

FROST

"Dandy."

"Any idea who might've tried to splatter you all over Pike's Place?"

"Jonathan Wainwright."

"Oh, goody. I'll just bop over and arrest his ass."

"Do that, would you?"

"Sure thing. On my way back should I pick up Sofia Vergara to wait on you hand and foot until you're up and around?"

"Even after I'm up and around." I told Sam what I'd found on Pear's desk and how I'd approached Wainwright.

"You tried to blackmail a United States Senator?"

"Of course not. I just warmly congratulated him on his deep, abiding love for children and offered to explain to the world how serious his commitment to them really is."

"And what, exactly, are you planning to do now?"

"Immediately, I going to try not to puke."

***

Daylight filtered through the thin hospital curtains. Chelsea sat beside the bed, her husband Charles stood at the foot.

"How are you?" she asked.

"Good. How's my dog?"

"Loud," Charles said.

"That's her job."

"Have you eaten?" Chelsea asked.

"No."

"I'll have the nurse bring you some breakfast."

Charles winced. "Hospital food is awful, Chelsea. There's a Starbucks across the way. Why don't you run over and grab us some decent coffee and a few breakfast muffins? I want to talk to Micah about the car."

Chelsea hesitated, then slung her purse over her shoulder. "I'll be back."

"I know you have a preference for older cars, Micah. I have a '76 Mercury parked in my garage," Charles said. Good condition, new white paint job. It belonged to Chelsea's mother, and nobody drives it. I've been meaning to sell it." He swallowed, pulled at his collar. "I had my mechanic go over it yesterday and drop a new battery into it. I know your car was destroyed, and I want to give you the Mercury."

"Charles, I can't--"

"Let me finish. I want you to take the car, and I want you to stay away from my family."

His words poured over me like molten lead.

"I like you, Micah. I respect you. You brought Kelly back to us and I know that I paid you, but I could never pay you enough." He paused. "That said, you scare the hell out of me."

"Charles--"

"Two hoodlums break into your house and try to kill you. The next day, somebody puts a bomb in your car and it's just luck you're the only one in the vicinity who got hurt. It's a wonder you're even alive.

"There is an armed policeman standing in front of your hospital door, for Christ's sake. Micah, I can't chance my wife or my daughter getting hurt or worse because they happened to be standing next to you at the wrong moment."

Charles pushed away from the foot of the bed, walked to the nightstand. He reached into his coat pocket, placed a set of

FROST

keys, a Certificate of Ownership and a parking stub on the tabletop.

"You know I'll respect your wishes, Charles. If you sold the car how much would you ask for it?"

"I don't know. A couple of thousand, maybe."

"I'll send you a check for twenty-five hundred."

"That isn't necessary."

"It's necessary if I'm to maintain any sense of self-respect."

Charles pushed his right hand in my direction. I shook it, once, let it go.

"We'll keep the dog until you're ready to care for it, again."

"Thanks."

"Life is hard. I'm very sorry, Micah."

"So am I, Charles. Take care."

"You, too." Charles turned and walked out of the room. I was alone, again.

FROST

Chapter Eighteen

I released myself from the hospital late Wednesday afternoon. Dr. Bierman was less than amused and refused to give me another penlight.

Donna Trent retrieved the Mercury from the parking garage. She refused to let me drive, so I let her ferry me to West Seattle. She parked on the street, took my arm and guided me up the tier of concrete steps that led to the entranceway.

The picture window on the front of the house now boasted three nailed sheets of plywood instead of glass.

"Your neighbors must absolutely love you," Donna said.

"Not to mention my landlord."

I unlocked the door and stepped inside. There is a feeling of warmth that embraces you when you step into your own home, a sense of security and joy and belonging. There was only emptiness here.

The house died.

I watched the dust dance inside the autumn sunbeams. A girl I might have had a future with had been taken away from me.

My best friend had been taken away from me.

My fears for her safety had taken my dog away from me.

My car, a car that fit me like the seat of a pair of eight-year-old Levi's had been taken from me.

My brother's mere presence had yet one more time torn away most everything of real importance in my life.

"Micah?" Donna said, quietly. "Are you okay?"

FROST

I realized I'd focused on the choreography before me and drifted. "I will be," I said. "Are you trustworthy?"

"Of course not."

"I'll have to trust you, anyway." I walked into the bedroom and opened my closet. "I'm going to put some clothes on the bed. There is a leather bag in the back. It would be most helpful if you'd pack the bag for me."

"And I'll try to keep the contents to myself," Donna said.

"Actually, I'd prefer to keep the contents."

Donna smiled, reached past me and pulled the satchel from the closet. She tossed it on the bed, unzipped the side panel, and gasped when the cash fell out.

"Don't trust banks?" she said, finally.

"Didn't need another toaster."

"If you don't mind my asking, how much is here?"

"Twenty-five thousand dollars. It's my emergency fund."

"Everything you have in this world, right?"

"I wouldn't go that far."

"Money, clothes, new car--are you leaving town?"

"Something like that. I need a safe place to heal for a day or two."

"The hospital--"

"It isn't safe there, and if I stayed it might not be safe for some of the other people there, either."

"You're welcome to stay with me, Micah."

"Thanks, but that puts you and Matt in the line of fire."

"Where will you go?"

"I can't tell you."

FROST

Donna folded a couple of pairs of jeans and several cotton crewneck sweaters. "Socks? Underwear? On second thought, I'd bet you don't wear underwear with jeans."

"Perceptive."

"The butt in your jeans wore without a panty line."

"You've been looking at my butt?"

"Don't flatter yourself. I looked at the pants I just folded."

I laughed a little, and the room curved around me. I sat down on the bare mattress.

"You're going to kill him, aren't you?"

"I hope so."

"Because if you don't he'll kill you."

"And possibly a good many other people."

"Cops won't get him, will they?"

I shook my head.

Donna sat on the bed beside me. "What can I do to help?"

"You could help me get a shower. I'm feeling really grungy."

Donna's lips curled into a smirk. "Are you making a pass at me, Frost?"

"Not until I've had a chance to look at the butt of your jeans."

Donna patted my knee and walked into the bathroom.
I lay back on the bed, heard the sound of running water and closed my eyes. I awoke naked, Donna gently rubbing my dirty hands. "C'mon, sport. Bath time." She walked me into the bathroom and lowered me into the tub.

"I said a shower."

"You can't sit up on the bed by yourself. What makes you think you can stand up in a shower?"

FROST

"Blind optimism."

"Where do you keep the shampoo?" I pointed to the cabinet under the sink. Donna lathered my hair, careful to avoid the newly stitched area of my scalp. She soaped a washcloth and scrubbed away at the bed grime and iodine, then rinsed, grabbed a can of shaving creme and a razor and shaved my face.

"You're very good at this," I said.

"Don't get used to it."

"Damn. And we were getting along so well."

Donna lowered her hand into the water and between my legs. She squeezed, gently. "Don't mess with me, sport. And by the way, I usually get dinner before my date gets undressed."

"I'll try to remember that in the future."

Donna helped me up, dried me off and walked me into the bedroom. I pulled on jeans and a sweatshirt, slipped into socks and a pair of black penny loafers and stood up.

"I need you to help me get downstairs."

"Just tell me what you need. I'll find it for you."

"No, you won't. We'll take it slow."

Donna helped me down the basement stairs. I found the hidden latch on the chimney and opened the panel, removed two of the Colts and dropped a full clip into each one of them. "Do you know how to use one of these?"

"I do."

"Take this," I said, shoving the gun toward her, grip first.

Donna palmed the little gun, held it as if she might try to guess the thing's weight. "Thanks, I guess."

I handed her a soft tanned leather holster. "Drop it into your purse and keep it with you. Don't hesitate to use if the situation warrants." I tossed her an extra clip. "Just in case.

FROST

When I get it back, I'm counting the bullets. You shoot somebody, you pay for the ammo."

"Cheap bastard."

"That's why you didn't get dinner."

FROST

Chapter Nineteen

Donna dropped me off at the corner of Third and Pine.
I waited, watched her drive off toward the Space Needle and then walked to Fourth Avenue, turned toward Westlake Center and ambled toward the Mayflower Hotel.

Clark Kent was too obvious, so was Bruce Wayne. I registered as Barry Allen, paid five days in advance in cash, and left instructions that I was not to be disturbed.

I let a bellhop carry my single leather satchel. She was the first female bellhop I'd ever encountered. She told me she was a sophomore at the University of Washington, and babbled incessantly about the vast opportunities for tourism the city offered. She opened the door to my room, pointed out the bathroom and the stunted refrigerator. I tipped her twenty dollars hoping to shut her up.

The windows afforded a view of Fourth Avenue and Stewart Street, immediately, Puget Sound and West Seattle a bit farther away. I gazed at the evening crowd, business people post-dinner and drinks, camera-toting tourists, and kids.

Kids. Lots of kids. Kids on skateboards, kids on bicycles, kids sitting on the curb. Kids holding hands, kids with arms wrapped around each other's waists, kids with faces plastered to one another seemingly sucking the life from each other's lips. Kids in high heels and too much makeup, hips cocked in an insane caricature of seduction, shirts cropped to reveal flat tummies or unbuttoned to reveal barely-there cleavage.

FROST

I closed the curtain and kicked off the penny loafers. I checked the lock on the door, slid the Ruger under a pillow and stretched out fully clothed across the comforter.

***

I felt rather than saw the sunlight punch the backside of the curtain. I sat up, waited for the room to stop spinning, then found my way into the tiny bathroom. I washed my face and brushed my teeth, edged to the midget refrigerator. I opened a can of Diet Pepsi and unwrapped a Hershey bar, settled into a padded straight-backed chair and ate breakfast.

I purposely neglected Bierman's prescription for codeine. The tear at the base of my skull throbbed. I'd been told to keep the stitches dry, but I wanted a shower so I tore the plastic cover from a drinking tumbler--sealed, as it were, for my protection--and wrapped the shield around my neck. I figured it would slide away the moment it faced the force of showering water.

I slithered out of my wrinkled clothing, tied the bag into a knot at my throat and stepped into the steaming cascade. I showered, gradually turned the hot water off until I stood chattering under a frigid torrent.

I pulled on faded blue jeans, a relaxed cut but ironed with a crisp seam in the center of both legs, eased a black turtleneck shirt over my head and around the stitches. I pulled on the shoulder holster and picked up my leather bomber jacket.

I grabbed two one dollar bills from my billfold, folded one bill into quarters and laid it along the inside of the door frame. I set the top of the bill at exactly the length of the other dollar bill as measured from the carpet, then closed the door to my room and

FROST

locked it. Anyone entering my room would most likely think a buck had fallen out of my pocket and not realize the thing was a makeshift security device--if the bill was gone or moved, somebody had been inside the room during my absence. I folded the other dollar and put it into the watch pocket of my jeans.

I paid too much for a pair of brand name aviator glasses at a kiosk inside Westlake Mall. I knew from experience it would be a short period of time before I either smashed them or lost them, so that lifetime warranty against scratching and warping was of absolutely no use to me, but I liked the way they sat on my face.

I bought a cup of coffee and found my way to a back table, pulled out my cellphone and turned it back on. Voicemail informed me that Miles and Donna wanted to know if I was all right. My landlord wanted me to know I had thirty days to vacate the premises and that he expected me to reimburse him for the damage to the house. A computer consultant with a Nigerian accent informed me that my computer had been stricken with a virus and that I needed to contact him immediately. My research contact in California had the information I'd requested on StoneVentures.

Chelsea wanted to know where the fuck I was, and how dare I team up with Charles to decide what particular associations she'd be allowed to participate in, demanded that I *call me on my cellphone you son-of-a-bitch because that's the one I answer directly, and I hope you're okay, Micah.*

I punched the speed-dial number for my researcher and arranged for him to email an encrypted copy of the information to Miles.

I called Miles, then Donna, assured their safety, assured them of mine, wouldn't tell them where I was. I promised to check

FROST

my voicemail several times a day and promised to return all of their calls.

I glanced at my watch, then called Sam Rollins. His voicemail told me to leave a message, and I did, told him I'd get back to him.

I punched in the number for Chelsea's cellphone. A recorded voice informed me the cellular number I had dialed was no longer a working extension. I smiled, should have known Charles would have structured that change.

Charles was a very thorough man.

I left Westlake Mall, grabbed a taxi, and had him take me to the Kickin' Boot Whiskey Kitchen on Shilshole. There wasn't much chance of running into my regular crowd there and I knew I needed some solid food in my system. A blonde girl in a black cowboy hat and enough silver and turquoise to outfit most of the remaining Navaho in North America took my order: the Butcher's Steak with baked potato and seasoned vegetables and kindly keep that blue cheese fondue off the plate and in the kitchen. I ate the steak and the potato, pushed the vegetables off to the side of the platter, and drank another ginger ale with the meal. I asked for coffee, ordered a Texas Brisket sandwich to go and asked the cowgirl to call me a taxi.

The taxi driver was sullen and surly, and frankly that suited me just fine. I made him take the scenic route back to downtown and climbed out two blocks away from the Mayflower.

I made certain no one followed me, ducked into Westlake Center Mall and made my way to the Mayflower's connecting corridor. The dollar bill perched at just the right height, but I'd had a rough week, so I palmed the Ruger, unlocked the door, and quickly confirmed my aloneness before laying the gun on the bed.

FROST

I slept fitfully, dreams filled with children and fat men and undraped women pleading for solace. Rapunzel floated through the visions, unfettered auburn tresses gently wrapping around her naked torso. I knew her, called to her, but she pulled away as I grabbed for her. Her skull split and black ink poured across her delicate face, filled her crystal eyes and gentle mouth, covered her breasts and belly. My own hand held the inked brush and thick, ebony fluid sprayed from the soaked bristles.

I awoke with a start. Dawn eased across the Sound, slipped under the curtain's hem. I climbed out of bed, pulled a cardboard cup of instant coffee from the refrigerator and turned on the television.

Steven Cook blandly informed me of more terrorist activity in the Middle East, more fighting among the various factions of what had once been a united Syria, another London bombing attributed to ISIL. I thought about the house on Halleck for a moment and realized I understood the concept of killing the messenger.

I drank the powdery coffee and took another shower. True to their word, the Mayflower staff had left my room undisturbed, so I re-used yesterday's towel.

I dressed, same basic outfit, but with a burgundy turtleneck under the bomber jacket. I rigged the door and walked to Lowell's for breakfast.

Lowell's was my usual breakfast destination and the hostess was an old friend. "We'd better put you in the back," Lola said. "Can't have somebody shooting out the window glass."

"I can find a back booth. Coffee on?"

"You know where it is. Are you eating?"

"Just get me the usual, hon."

FROST

"Don't call me *hon.*"

I moseyed upstairs and found a back booth, stopped on the way to grab a mug and fill it with coffee. Lola sauntered over and asked how I was doing. I told her I was okay and asked if anyone had been in looking for me.

She said no, not that she knew of.

I ate my meal, laid a twenty on the table and left. I walked to Fifth Avenue, turned past the Westin and into the Enterprise Rent-a-Car lot. I paid for the use of a black Hyundai Santa Fe for five days and made sure to buy the insurance. The Santa Fe had all the personality of a generic can of peas, but that might work to my advantage. I pulled on my new aviator sunglasses and hoped for anonymity.

I drove to West Lee, parked in front of Pear's place. The house was dark, the BMW gone. There was nothing there I needed at this particular moment, so I hit the ignition switch and pulled away. I drove past Chelsea's, past Donna's, sped along Highway 99 until I reached the house I rented in West Seattle.

I emptied the hidey-holes, bagged Pear's address book and all the flashdrives. I tucked the Ruger into a vinyl pouch and sealed it, then grabbed one of the Colts and shoved it into a holster and stuck it behind my belt. I grabbed the last of the cash I'd hidden in the house--another twenty-five thousand--then walked to the linen closet.

I slid the false panel from the wall, opened the metal case inside the cubby hole and removed a passport, driver's license, a concealed carry permit, an American Express Gold Card and a checkbook wrapped in plastic with an ATM Card. The checking account boasted ten thousand dollars under the name Hal Jordan, the same moniker on the identification and the credit card. All

FROST

were valid, set up some time ago. I used them just often enough to maintain viability. I recovered a leather wallet, inserted the checkbook, the bank cards and the ID into it, then tucked it and the calfskin-bound passport into my bomber jacket's inside pocket.

I eased downstairs, took a long look at Rapunzel. I wished I had time to work on her, to give life to the unfinished drawing, but I didn't. She might well be the best penciled work I'd ever done. I hoped I'd see her again, hoped I'd be able to finish her.

I locked up, pulled away from the house. It was almost noon. I drove back to town, parked the car in the Mayflower's underground garage, then slept the day away.

I got up just before midnight. I took the elevator to the garage, drove the car down First Avenue through town and turned off onto the Harbor Island Bridge. Halfway across, I gunned the engine, jerked the wheel to the right and crashed through the guardrail, left the flat driving surface and plunged into the cold, dark water of Puget Sound.

FROST

Chapter Twenty

I'd opened the Santa Fe's windows before leaving the driving through the guardrail.

My billfold was safely tucked into the inside pocket of the bomber jacket, and I craftily caught the coat sleeve in the passenger door so the thing wasn't washed away by rushing water. The ID could be easily replaced down the road, but I'd miss the jacket. I unclipped the chamois holster from the small of my back and tossed the Colt into the glove box. I pulled off one of my penny loafers and left it jammed under the brake pedal.

The water was halfway up my torso, moving much more slowly than I expected. I took several deep breaths, exhaled. I glanced at my left wrist and cursed, realized I'd forgotten to take off my collectable Mickey Mouse Seiko.

A drowned rat has little appeal, and I hoped there wouldn't be two of us.

I took a deep breath and held it.

The Santa Fe slipped beneath the Sound. Water rose about the bridge of my nose, past my eyes

I grabbed the steering wheel and pulled myself toward the open window. My shoulders jammed, but I hunched them toward my chest, pushed away from the steering wheel and made it through the window.

I swam toward the surface, broke into the open air, gasped for breath. I looked around, spotted the old abandoned Fisher Mill in the distance and started to swim.

FROST

I pushed as hard as I could. It wouldn't be long before SPD got a boat here and I needed to be clear of the area before they arrived. I swam, tried not to raise much of a splash in the brackish water. My arms began to ache and so did my head, and the cold water sucked at my legs. Numbness seeped into most of my body. Scummy water pushed into my nostrils and when I choked water filled my open mouth.

I trolled onward, finally reached the shore.

Miles saw me, reached over the side of the loading dock for my hand. He pulled me over the wood plank, handed me a towel. "Mr. Jordan, I presume?"

FROST

Chapter Twenty-One

The suit was navy blue, conservative and dull, the trousers unpleated. The collar of the simple white shirt lay flat alongside medium width lapels. The regimental club tie combined with plain black oxfords, effectively presenting the image of a dork.

Miles removed the stitches, covered the base of my skull with some sort of liquid stitch, then cut my hair above the ears and off the collar, in effect a sanitized military brush cut. He trimmed the moustache to a severe hard slash of neatly groomed whiskers. I pushed red horn-rimmed spectacles up the bridge of my nose, gazed into the looking glass and didn't recognize myself.

I picked up the black leather passbook, opened it, studied the ID. My photograph sat alongside a holographic shield, the words *Federal Bureau of Investigation* floating in blue beneath it. I'd had occasion to peer at several of these over the years and I couldn't see any variations between this one and those. The legend beneath the shield identified me as a Special Investigations Officer and included a printed *V* under the rank.

"What's this?" I asked, pointed at the *V*.

"It's a Roman numeral five. Your security clearance."

"Until somebody requests an ID verification."

"D.C. shows you as an active SI-V."

"Excuse me?"

"The FBI databank requires a designated security code for ID verification. If anybody checks, you're for real."

"You're kidding me."

FROST

"I programmed the FBI Operations bank to issue the ID and the verification code, then to abort the issue directive. You'll check out, but your record won't be accessible. Anybody checking will probably assume it's classified."

"How'd you get into the system?"

"Nothing personal, Micah, but you wouldn't be able to begin to be able to understand the process. That's what you pay me for, remember?"

I traced my fingertip across the edge of the ID card. "What else can you hack into?"

Miles grinned. "Let's just say you'd better be nice to me."

Serena knocked on the door, walked into the room. "You're on television, Micah."

We all shuffled into the living room. Steven Cook deadpanned the news of a car skidding out of control the night before and tumbling into the water around Harbor Island. "The car had been rented to local artist and sometime private investigator Micah Frost. You may remember that Frost was hospitalized last weekend when his car exploded at Pike's Place Market. A spokesperson for Swedish Hospital reports that Frost checked himself out of the hospital against the advice of his doctors several days ago. The body has not yet been recovered and Seattle Police are withholding comment at this time."

"You look remarkably well for a dead man," Miles said.

Serena giggled. "You look like a geek."

"Does this mean you won't go out with me?'

"I might," Serena smiled, "but I'm expensive."

"You're hanging around Miles too much."

"Don't be picking on Uncle Miles."

"*Uncle* Miles?"

FROST

Miles sighed. "I couldn't move an unrelated young lady in here, Micah. I have an image to maintain."

***

The Time's City Room was something of a disappointment. I'd come in looking for crowded bustle and instead found four neat rows of cubicles nearly devoid of people. I found an Editor's Desk and asked for Donna Trent.

"She's in a meeting," the woman snapped.

I reached inside the breast pocket of my coat, retrieved the FBI passbook, tossed the opened case on her desk. "Maybe you can get her out of it."

She looked at the badge card and grimaced, picked up the telephone receiver on her desk. I didn't listen to what she phrased, but she hung up the phone and told me to follow her. The woman led me through the City Room to a small conference hall and told me to wait inside.

I was looking through the window when Donna came in. The reflection in the glass told me she was alone.

"Inspector Jordan?"

"Please close the door." I heard the latch click. "Thank you for seeing me, Ms. Trench."

"Trench?"

I turned around, stripped the glasses away from my face.

Donna's eyes were raw. She stared at me for a long, silent moment, and then walked across the room to where I stood. "You son-of-a-bitch," she growled, and rammed her right fist just below my navel. Donna had an excellent understanding of the concept and execution of the sucker punch. I doubled over gasping for air.

FROST

Donna took a deep breath, held it for a moment, blew it out slowly through open teeth. "I feel better," she said.

"G-g-good," I wheezed.

"I think I need a drink."

"I think I need a doctor."

"Get a grip, *Jordan*."

***

"Two Bloody Mary's, both doubles," Donna told the waiter. "And on the way back, find somebody who looks like they need the celery and give it to them."

"You remembered."

"Don't talk to me. I'll tell you when you can talk to me."

"Donna--"

"Shut the fuck up."

We drank the first round and Donna ordered another. We drank that round and she ordered a third.

"You can talk to me, now," she said, "but you'd damned well better be polite."

"Yes, ma'am."

"I wouldn't recommend sarcasm."

I smiled my most sincere smile. Her expression didn't change.

"I'm glad you're alive, but I might have to kill you."

"I understand."

"You don't understand shit. Why did you do this to me? Why did you put me through this?"

"I was afraid you were being watched."

"So what."

FROST

"You know the kind of people who'd be watching. Any indication my death was an act, you would have been in danger, and Matt as well. If anyone was watching, your honest reaction bought you freedom and safety."

Donna raised her hand, snapped her finger at the waiter, waved her index finger in the universal gesture for one more time. He nodded. She slumped down into the booth. "I wish I had a cigarette."

"They'll kill you, you know."

"I wanted it for you." The waiter brought the next round and cleared the empties from the table. "Who else knows?"

"Miles."

"I'll kill him, too."

"How's Matt?"

"Upset."

"Miles knew all along?"

"I needed his help."

"And now you want mine."

"Well, we are in this together."

Donna chugged the rest of her drink. "Okay, but I don't want any more surprises from you."

I reached into my pocket and retrieved a small manila envelope. "These are a couple of action shots of a certain United States Senator. As a hotshot reporter I figure you'd have an interest in Wainwright's explanation."

"Where'd I get them?"

"Micah Frost gave them to you, sealed, with instructions to open in the event of his death."

***

FROST

Steven Cook looked at the ID and fought to retain his professionally bland expression. "What can I do for you, Mr. Jordan?"

"You can start by explaining your relationship with David Welsh."

"I don't know a David Welsh."

"Do you know a Pearson Stone?"

"No."

"How long have you had an interest in fucking children?"

The color in Cook's face bled below his shirt collar. "Get out of my office."

I picked up the passbook, tucked it into my coat pocket. I turned, grabbed a chair and pulled it toward the desk. I sat down, propped my feet up on the desktop and crossed them at the ankles. "You've got a serious problem, Cook."

Cook picked up the telephone receiver. "I'm calling my attorney."

"Good idea. You complete that call and you'll literally *be* the six o'clock news."

Cook punched at the number pad.

"If I walk out of this office without getting what I came for the News Director here gets a full set of eight-by-ten color glossies of you and a young lady who should've spent that time doing her sixth grade homework."

Cook cursed aloud as he slammed the telephone receiver into its cradle.

"Stone, now. I am not a patient man."

"I don't know him."

"Baby-pokers don't do well in prison, Cook. The glossies in my pocket will put you there for a long, long time."

FROST

"I don't--"

"You'll be a very old man with very little bowel control." I pushed the red spectacles up the bridge of my nose. "Assuming, of course, that some overzealous butt-fucker doesn't kill you bouncing the top of your head against the cement cell wall."

Cook swallowed, sank into his chair.

"I won't ask again."

"I met him in California when I was with KBLA."

"How long ago?"

"Eight, nine years."

"How? Where?"

"Party. Yes, one of those parties, alcohol, dope--" Cook paused-- "girls."

"Little girls."

"Little girls."

"Go on."

"It was like a club, you know? I mean these kids were on the street, they were active anyway. Stone did them a favor, took care of them, kept them safe."

"Your conception of safe and mine vary considerably. You just assumed a twelve or thirteen year old child was capable of making that sort of a career choice."

"I didn't think about it."

"I'll bet."

"In some cultures--"

"Finish that sentence and you will not leave this room alive."

We sat in silence for a moment.

"Where else does Stone keep houses?"

FROST

"Los Angeles, San Francisco, Las Vegas, Tokyo, London. Hell he's got houses in most every major city."

"All kids."

"I guess. I don't know."

"Who killed Camey Horne?"

"I don't know."

"But you did know her."

"I knew her."

"In the Biblical sense?"

"She's a little old for me."

"I took my feet off of his desk and stood up. "You wouldn't know anything about a computer file with a customer list and some confidential banking information?"

"How would I know anything about that?"

"You're more than just one of Stone's customers. I'm not exactly sure how you fit into all of this, but I'll figure it out."

"You're wrong."

"Of course I am." I turned around and walked out of Cook's office.

***

I met Miles at 13 Coins. We both ordered the Chicken Fried Steak and, thanks to my over-indulgence with Donna earlier, no alcohol.

"What are we going to do with Serena?" Miles asked after the waitress walked away.

I unfolded the cloth napkin and draped it across my lap. I gazed around the room for a moment, then said, "I don't know,

Miles. You've been with her a couple of days, how does she seem to you?"

"Very adult. She's been through a great deal for a girl her age. Oh, and she's fifteen, barely, not sixteen."

"Oh, goody."

"Maybe you could set her and the boy up at Donna's as roommates."

"That could work. You could be the housemother."

"Do I look like Donna Reed?"

"You've got the wiggle for it."

"That's what I've been told. Seriously, we need to give this some thought."

"I have an idea, but I haven't figured out how to set it up."

"Tell me."

"Serena just wants a normal life. Ideally, we could get her into school somewhere."

"We?"

"We, Uncle Miles."

"I should have known that would come back and bite me in the butt."

"How bright do you think Serena is?"

Miles shrugged. "Bright enough. I could run her over to Central Community College and have her quizzed. The guidance counselor is a close friend."

"What's his name?"

"Karen Price."

"Get her over there. Let's find out if her scores are good enough for a GED."

"Hell, I can hack into the E.D. system and have them issue her a GED."

FROST

"The paper's no good if she doesn't have the skill to back it up."

"I see your point. I'll set it up."

"And the boy as well?"

"Matt? Good idea."

"You don't really expect him to qualify for a GED, too?"

"No, but it would be helpful to know what grade he should be in."

The waitress brought dinner and we ate, rapidly devoured the meat and a pile of mashed potatoes. Miles ordered pecan pie, I settled for black coffee.

"What did you find in the stuff from Devin?"

"Devin is much too thorough. I've only been able to wade through about half of what he sent. StoneVentures is home based out of San Bernardino, actually. It's mostly middleman kind of stuff, representing foreign buyers for American goods and negotiating bulk purchase prices from the American producers. They don't actually stock anything, everything is shipped directly to the overseas customer."

"Why wouldn't the foreign buyer just buy the stuff on their own?"

"Well, first the buyer has to identify the producer, not always an easy task if you're halfway around the. Then, you have to try and determine which producer has the better quality product, and then you have to negotiate a reasonable price. Most American companies don't hesitate to escalate the purchase point when dealing with a foreign buyer who doesn't have good access to comparative pricing. Assuming you get that far, you still have to walk your goods through the labyrinth of Import and Export regulations, both this country's and your own.

FROST

"What StoneVentures does is pretty simple, really. Say I'm a Taiwanese or Japanese businessman who wants to purchase a million dollars of say, computer chips. I call Stone's outfit, tell them what I want and how much I'm willing to spend. For ten percent of the budget, plus tariffs and shipping, StoneVentures gets me my chips and the supplier usually doesn't know he's dealing with an overseas buyer until he gets the ship-to address. I don't have to do anything but sign the check and count the goods when they arrive.

"However--and this is important--StoneVentures combines my order with orders from other clients and negotiates a cheaper bulk price than I'll ever know about. It doesn't matter much, because the price I'm quoted is better than anything I could have done on my own, so by consolidating the ten grand commission on my million dollar purchase becomes closer to, say, a forty thousand dollar commission. I'm still paying import and export fees and shipping expenses, so the forty grand Stone makes is all company profit."

"Is StoneVentures viable?"

"Very. Stone reported a company gross income of some nine billion dollars last year."

"Nine billion?"

Miles nodded. "And there's more. A lot of real estate worldwide, all in the company's name. There's a client list that includes a number of North Koreans and Middle Easterners, and Russians, too, but it's unclear just exactly what Stone does for them."

"If Stone has that kind of money coming in, why mess with this kiddie stuff?"

"I don't know."

FROST

Chapter Twenty-Two

"Wainwright denied it, of course. Said the pictures were forgeries and he'd sue the paper if we published them."

Hal Jordan had checked into the Fairmont Olympic Hotel. "I expected that, but I also expect Wainwright will get ahold of Pear and demand he clean up his security problem. If I can force Pear into stirring up a hornet's nest, he might just get stung."

"We can hope." Donna dropped onto the bed and stretched out, kicked off her shoes. "Did Miles find anything on those flashdrives yet?"

"More financial stuff. He's wading through it now trying to find anything we can use."

Donna turned on her side and propped up her arm, laid her head against her hand. "Do you think I'm attractive?"

I took a long, solid look at the woman on my bed. Donna's close cropped black hair curled around her eyes and cheeks. Thin lips perched beneath a short straight nose, slender shoulders sat above small, upturned breasts. The torso sloped to a tiny waist. He legs were long and thin, their shape nicely defined by the black denim wrapped around them. I could only see the front of her from where I sat, but I'd watched her walk in front of me the night I met her and I could attest a certain appreciation for the shape of her bottom and the manner in which it swayed.

"Why do you ask?"

"Vain curiosity."

"I don't find you attractive, Donna, I think you're actually quite beautiful."

"Do you think I'm a lesbian?"

"I hadn't really thought about it."

"I was wondering why you haven't made a pass at me, you know, other than the bump on your head which you seem to be over."

"Maybe I was afraid you'd turn me down."

"You don't strike me as someone who's had many women turn you down, and you certainly don't strike me as someone who'd be trounced by a single rejection."

"Wow."

"You're an interesting man, Micah. I'd be lying if I said I didn't feel a certain attraction to you."

"And what is that attraction, exactly?"

Donna pursed her lips. "I don't know, exactly. I appreciate complexity, and you may be the most complex person I've ever met. Miles told me what really happened the night those men broke into your home, and I can understand why you did what you did, maybe even condone it." She bit at her thumb. "Your determination to act on your own convictions is somewhat exciting."

"On the excitement scale what I do is about halfway between a visit to the dentist and a haircut."

"Don't try that act on me, Frost. I've seen you up close."

"I don't think I'm much different from anybody else, Donna."

"I think you are. Most of us are far too willing to compromise, Micah, in too much of a hurry to overlook those things we know aren't right and let somebody else handle the dirty work, but you won't, or can't, do that. You'll do the work, fix the problem any way you can and accept the consequences, even if what you have to do is against the law."

FROST

"Law doesn't interest me, much. I do have an occasional interest in justice."

"Like I said."

"I just do what I have to do."

"I might have something for you to do."

I chose my words carefully. "Donna, you and I have become friends. You are an incredibly beautiful and intelligent woman and I have to admit I like the notion of you attracted to me, but I am hardly in any position to offer any kind of a romantic relationship."

"Is there someone you're involved with?"

I thought briefly of Chelsea, but that wasn't allowed. "No, there isn't."

"You said you weren't in love with Camey Horne."

"No. I might've been, eventually, but no."

"Well, then, Mr. Frost, I suggest you join me between these sheets here and now so I can get the thought of it out of my mind and concentrate on the other things I need to focus on."

***

The bedsheets tangled about us. I leaned against the headboard and Donna draped across my chest.

"You've got some interesting scars," she said.

I gazed down at her tousled hair, lightly grabbed a handful of it. "You've got some very interesting moves."

"My mother's fault. She made a point of telling me that sex was something one should learn to be very, very good at."

"Next time you talk to her, give her my thanks."

"I'll do that."

FROST

My cellphone rang. Only two people knew the number of the burner I'd acquired and one of them lay naked and delicious on my bed. I punched the thing and said, "Hello, Miles."

"Serena is gone."

I pushed Donna off me, sat up and reached for a pair of jeans. "What do you mean, gone?"

"I mean she's not here. I had to go out a while ago and when I got back she was gone."

"Any chance she left on her own?"

"I don't think so, she didn't have anywhere to go. And, I don't think she'd have left without her new wardrobe."

"I'm on the way. Call me if she shows or if you hear from her before I get there." I punched the end-call button and turned to Donna. "Where is Matt?"

"He's at my sister's."

"Call her." I tossed my phone in Donna's general direction. "Make sure they're both okay."

Donna punched at the keypad. "I don't like this."

"I don't either."

Matt was fine. Donna's sister lived out in Kirkland and she'd taken the boy there so he didn't have to be alone while Donna did her job. Donna made certain DeDe had my burner number and rang off.

"Get dressed," I said.

The Fairmont to Mile's Capitol Hill apartment is a fifteen minute run. We made it in eight, which included the elevator ride to the parking garage. Miles waited for us, looked out of place clutching the little .25 automatic I'd left with him. He gritted his teeth, nodded toward the room Serena had claimed as her own.

FROST

Donna took his hand, squeezed it, and followed me into the girl's room.

Serena's new clothing hung neatly in the closet. Underwear folded into a bureau drawer, barely used cosmetics lined the space in front of the dresser's mirror. A pair of leather oxfords and a pair of new Nikes tucked under the foot of the bed. Miles had made a gift of a small hand-tooled leather purse to the girl, one of those things not much larger than a can of cola, and when I opened it two twenty dollar bills, a fiver and a couple of ones floated to the carpet.

If Serena had left of her own volition, she might have abandoned whatever clothes she couldn't walk around in, but she'd been on the street before and she understood the concept of monetary necessity.

"How long were you out, Miles?"

"I don't know. An hour, maybe a bit longer. What are we going to do?"

"Check with the neighbors, check up and down the street, see if anyone remembers seeing the girl in the last hours or so. Print a couple of the headshots we used to annoy Wainwright, show them around. And keep your phone turned on. Donna, you go with him, and both of you carry your guns."

"What are you going to do?"

"Better if you don't know." I squeezed Miles' shoulder. "It'll be okay."

"I'm sorry, Micah."

"Not your fault. Apparently, I wasn't as careful as I thought I was."

"We don't know that," Donna said.

"Yeah, I think we do."

143

FROST

I found the Mercury a block away from the apartment, exactly where Miles had left it. I climbed inside, fired it up and screeched away from the curb, barreled down Broadway to John Street, spun, aimed toward Seattle Center. I rammed through the shopping quarter of Queen Anne, shot up the hill and whipped onto West Lee.

Pear's house stood dark, apparently empty. I shoved the Mercury into the driveway, scrambled out of the car. I ran to the back of the house, grasped the kitchen doorknob and turned it, found it locked. I stepped back, planted my left foot parallel to the door, spun, shoved my weight onto my right foot and rammed it just beneath the doorknob. The frame splintered and I kicked again, two, three, four times, and the thing swung loose. I palmed the Ruger and stepped inside.

A quick swing through the house confirmed its immediate vacancy.

It was just after ten, and I knew I couldn't get into Pear's offices before morning. I thought for a moment, headed back to the Mercury.

The Halleck monstrosity was twenty minutes away. I headed toward the Highway 99 Viaduct, skidded into the outside lane and punched the accelerator pad. The Mercury roared into the night, a white charger questing to the Grail.

The house was dark. I stopped the car in front, put on the emergency brake and stepped out of it. I palmed the Ruger, tossed the red horn-rimmed disguise onto the dashboard, then gobbled the concrete steps two at a time, oblivious to the clicking of my cowboy boot heels against the concrete.

A massive front door stood open and unlighted. I pushed inside, eased across the foyer and into the cavernous living room.

FROST

I felt, rather than heard something move. I dropped to the floor, waited a long moment, heard nothing. My eyes slowly adjusted to the darkness and I made the shape of a man in front of me swaying back and forth ever so slightly. "Don't move," I barked.

I eased myself up, the Ruger pointed away from me, climbed to my feet. My left hand found the wall switch and I thumped it. Light flooded the room.

David Welsh hovered before me, one end of an orange nylon boating cord knotted around Blondie's neck and the other end vanished over the open balcony of the upper floor. A series of burns covered his naked chest, and I knew from experience they'd been inflicted with a lighted cigarette. His eyes bulged, his swollen tongue filled his mouth and winked between his gaping lips. Blood soaked the cloth around the shattered kneecap and the leg hung at an odd angle as if the muscle roped around the thing had been sliced away.

Checking the house was a waste of time, but I did it anyway, gave the place a quick once over, didn't find anything or anybody. I thought briefly about calling the police, then thought better of it. The body would be rediscovered sooner than later and I could do without the inconvenience of explaining my own death until Hal Jordan accomplished what he'd set out to do.

I pulled a handkerchief out of my back pocket, wiped down the doorknob and the doorframe I'd touched when I came in. I pushed the Ruger back into its holster and left the house, fired up the Mercury and drove over the hill, turned and coasted to the beach. I parked the car and sat.

I gave it a few moments to see if anyone followed me, didn't see anyone, so I climbed out of the car and strolled to a

FROST

concrete piling and sat down. A brilliant moon lit the Sound. Someone had a fire blazing in one of the cement bunkers and the stench of burning pine tar stung my nostrils. Lovers strolled across the sandy expanse of beach, fingers intertwined, arms wrapped around each other's waists, heads folded onto shoulders or laps. I remembered a night not so long ago with my own arms wrapped around a lady I'd looked forward to knowing. I gazed at a couple settled against a piece of driftwood, flesh melded into one being Siamese twins attached at the heart.

A ferry horn sounded in the distance. I lifted my gaze, noted the ship cruising toward Vashon. I wondered for a moment if I could learn to tolerate the enforced solitude dictated by island living, quickly decided I probably could.

Why would Pear order an underling killed in a house that was easily connected to him? Camey Horne murdered in his own home and Blondie tortured and murdered in a house newly acquired by his company. The cops would have a heyday once they ran a title check.

And why take Serena? It made no sense.

I watched the sound for a while, wished for a decent cup of hot coffee. I checked my cellphone, but there were no messages.

Something slammed behind my eyes, a force of light bathed the inside sockets. I shook my head, put my hand to my face. I covered my eyes, saw one of the professionals at Pike's Place Market twirl a lit cigarette and shove the fiery end into the vinyl top of my late Dodge.

I held no admiration for Pear, but I recognized the canny intellect he'd displayed in building his complicated and intertwined, not to mention profitable, operation. Pear certainly wouldn't order Blondie eliminated inside the Halleck house, he'd

FROST

run him out to one of the islands or into the basement of some waterfront warehouse to do it. He might even have pull Blondie out of state.

I knew Pear to be quite capable of murder, and I knew that firsthand, but self-preservation was his primary concern, always had been, always would be.

Pear would have sent Blondie, Bozo and Dick Dastardly after me in a parking lot, but he wouldn't have sent them to kill me in my own home, and anyway, Blondie told me himself that the home invasion was his own idea, undoubtedly the result of a bruised ego. I could picture Pear's anger at the mere prospect of being connected to the dead clown and his compatriots.

Serena, the presumed under-aged pregnant result of a forced liaison with Wainwright was nowhere to be found, a situation obviously not of her own doing. Blondie, the jerk responsible for pulling Serena off the street and into service at the chicken ranch, hung as first tortured, then dead meat. Camey Horne, dead, the manner of her death--*Slowly, Sam Rollins said, and probably in a great deal of pain*--a vague suggestion of an extreme interrogation, a simple quest for information?

Maybe my own blind hatred of my sibling had clouded my judgement. Maybe I'd been focusing on the wrong end of this puzzle. Pear remained a slime ball in need of wiping away, but I realized now that my involvement in this mess probably initiated through another source.

Wainwright was the one with a personal interest in finding Serena.

Wainwright was the one who would've recognized Blondie's potential as a source of information concerning Serena's whereabouts.

FROST

I didn't know for a fact that Wainwright killed Camey Horne, or more likely had her killed, or why he would have done so, but I did know he'd sic'd two of his boys on me, boys he could easily access as a member of the Senate Armed Services and the Intelligence Committees, both on which he sat. And, he'd have easy access to classified information documenting involvement in covert activity directed by my father, activity utilizing two children as weaponry.

Wainwright would know Pear and I were brothers.

I slipped off the piling, brushed away the sand and walked back to my car. The night was young and I had promises to keep.

FROST

Chapter Twenty-Three

Drizzle covered the windshield. I punched the wiper button, allowed two swipes across the glass and turned it back off.

I drove through Birkenstock Lane, the nickname Miles bestowed upon Wallingford during a visit to the Wallingford Wurst Festival some years before. He'd been amazed at the number of old hippies we'd found wearing tie-died shirts over tattered jeans and appalled by the scores of clunky strapped sandals we encountered. "Feet are not the most attractive part of the human body," he'd said, "and those damned sandals have somehow been designed to emphasize every hideous twist of nail and bone and callous to be found beneath the ankle."

I remember Miles wearing heavy leather workboots that Saturday, thick waffle-soled wonders topped by bright green leather and yellow laces.

Almost Saturday midnight and Wallingford bustled. Bearded men and unbra'ed women filled the restaurants and pubs, college kids filled the arcade and the movie house. There is a Taco Bell of all things constructed entirely of chrome and glass and it filled with teenagers who apparently lacked the ability to understand that a baseball cap is worn with the bill above the eyebrows, not above the collar. BMWs and Volvos and Mercedes blended with Volkswagen Beetles, bicycles, skateboards and Metro busses, all bowing to the weekend priority of the pedestrian.

I drove through the overwhelming press of people and vehicles, found my way to Sunnydale Avenue and turned onto it. I glanced at my watch--a subtle Superman design with the Man of

FROST

Steel's face at three, Lois Lane's at six, Clark Kent's at nine and the triangular red *S* logo at twelve. I wasn't sure I'd find Dolly Michelle Grant Parton home at midnight on Saturday, but she was my next logical step, so I parked the car and tramped up the walkway.

The apartment was an elongated multiplex affair, eight single units fashioned from brick and monkey wood. Each had its own separate entrance, the door framed by a tiny front porch, and each opened onto not enough yard to speak of. I wondered idly if the tenants actually bought lawnmowers or just snipped at the green growth with scissors.

I walked down the dark sidewalk to Unit Six. Light peered from beneath curtains in the apartment's front room. I stepped onto the tiny porch and heard music inside. I knocked on the door.

The curtain rustled. The girl's face peered through the opening, and a moment later the porch light flashed on. The door opened just a crack. I could see the cheap door chain hanging in the opening.

"What do you want?"

"Michelle Grant?"

"Do I know you?"

I flashed the open passbook in front of the one eye that peered through the slit. "Hal Jordan, Federal Bureau of Investigation. I need to speak with you."

Her eyes sparked, widened. "What about?" The eye looked me up and down. "You don't look much like an FBI agent."

I glanced down at my jeans and scuffed cowboy boots. "Miss Grant, I either speak to you now or I can get a warrant and we can do this downtown. Which do you prefer?"

FROST

The door closed and I heard the chain unclick. "You might as well come in."

The apartment was tiny, but expensively furnished. A soft leather loveseat leaned against the main wall and two mahogany and fabric arm chairs sat across from them separated by a small bookcase. An oval coffee table perched in the center of the room, and the far wall boasted the biggest flat screen television I'd ever encountered.

Michelle stepped into the loveseat and curled her legs beneath her. Her thick blonde hair curled freely about her shoulders. She was barefoot, wore red sweatpants and a gym-grey sweatshirt, obviously unencumbered by undergarments.

"Miss Grant--Michelle, I apologize for the late hour, but there's a young girl's life at stake. I'll try to make this brief."

Her features twisted into a frown. "Young girl? What young girl, who?"

"Michelle, how do you know Pearson Stone?"

"I work for him."

"When did you last see him?"

"Friday. Yesterday."

"Where is he now?"

"I don't know."

"Michelle, please excuse my lack of tact, but Mr. Stone is involved in some things I don't believe you are even aware of, much less connected to. I think you're a nice young lady and everything we've been able to find out about you confirms that."

"You're investigating me?"

"We know you have more than a business relationship with Stone. He's been under surveillance for some time, both at his office and at his home." I paused, let *at his home* sink in. "You know that his partner was recently murdered."

"Pear wouldn't--"

"Ms. Horne hired a private investigator named Micah Frost to look into Stone's, shall we say, *under-the-counter* business operations. She didn't know that the two men are, or were, in fact brothers. Stone found out about his brother's investigation and, well, Frost died under suspicious circumstances less than a week ago."

"A car accident. I saw it on the news."

"We don't think it was an accident. Stone owns a house on Halleck Street just off of Alki Avenue and that house has been used exclusively for prostitution from the moment Stone bought it. A young man was murdered there tonight."

"Oh, god, no---"

"Before his death, Frost was able to remove a fifteen-year-old girl from the whorehouse on Halleck. The girl was a runaway, dragged off the street by Stone's people. She was held against her will, beaten, raped, forced to have sex with whomever she was thrown at. The girl wanted to help us stop this, Michelle, but about two hours ago she was stolen out from under us."

A single tear trailed down Michelle's cheek, but she kept her voice steady. "I didn't know."

"I believe you."

"What is the girl's name?"

"Serena. Where is Stone?"

"I don't know. He called me this afternoon and cancelled a date we had for tonight, but he didn't tell me where he was."

"Where do you think he might be?"

"Anywhere. Everywhere."

FROST

"Why did he cancel?"

"Pear never gives me a reason for anything he does. He's a very forceful person."

"You must have some idea of where he might go."

"Maybe. I mean, there are places I know he goes to, but he doesn't have any kind of a favorite or a routine. I could give you a list."

"Why don't you pull some clothes on and take me."

"That might not be such a good idea."

"If Stone finds out I've been here, it might not be safe for you."

"Pear wouldn't--"

"Michelle, we both know what kind of a man Pear Stone is. I knew the minute I got the case file and reviewed the surveillance footage. You knew the minute he tied a leather strap across your mouth and made you bleed."

The girl's lower lip quivered. Her shoulders slumped and she seemed to sink into the loveseat. "What do you want me to do?"

"Take me where you think Stone might go."

The girl looked at me. I could see thought dance behind her eyes, but I couldn't recognize the steps. "All right," Michelle said.

She pushed herself out of the loveseat and padded down the hallway, stepped into the bedroom and pulled the sweatshirt over her head. She didn't bother to close the door. It was neither the time, nor the place, but I wasn't able to tear my eyes away from her nakedness. The girl was lovely. She stepped out of the sweatpants, slid beyond where I could see her, stepped back into the doorway to pull on jeans. She opened a drawer, tugged a pink and white sweater over her head and then stepped back into the hallway carrying a pair of short blue boots. "There's a navy blue parka hanging in the closet," she said, nodded toward a door. "Would you grab it for me?"

I got up and opened the door. The parka hung with a tan raincoat and a couple of lightweight jackets. I pulled the coat from the hanger and held it as Michelle slid her arms into it.

Michelle was methodical, pointed me toward a half-dozen bars and restaurants, entered each establishment and cornered a particular barmaid or bartender, asked her question, left. I watched her repeat the process from Broadway to Ballard to Pioneer Square without any success.

We left 13 Coins in SeaTac just after four and drove back to town. Most of the clubs were closed now and Michelle didn't know where else to look other than at Pear's home. I aimed the Mercury toward Queen Anne and drove past the house on West Lee, found it still dark and deserted, the cobbled driveway empty.

Michelle remained quiet, curled into her seat, her hands knotted between her legs. I drove back to Wallingford and parked in front of her brick abode. "Do you have someplace you can stay?"

"Do you think that's necessary?"

"Until I can pick up Stone. I can put you in the Westin for a few days until we can this sorted out. No fuss, just a couple of days of vacation. You won't be locked away and you'll have access to downtown. We'll give you some spending money and pick up all the bills, of course."

"Guess this means I'm out of a job."

"Don't worry about it. The bureau will make sure you're solvent until you can find somewhere else you'd like to be."

FROST

"Am I going to have to testify or something? Are you coming after me, too? I didn't know anything about any of this, I swear."

"I won't ask you to testify."

"What then?"

"I want the girl Serena back safe and sound, and I want you safe until I can get Stone handcuffed in the back seat of my car. Then, we can all get on with our lives."

The girl leaned her head against the headrest. "Let's do it."

We walked to Michelle's front door. She gave me the key and we stepped inside. She vanished down the short hallway, packed a leather workout bag.

"Does Stone have a key to this place?"

"Yes, he does. Why?"

"I'd like to hold on to your key for a day or two."

Michelle shrugged. "Why not? I'm not coming back until you tell me I can."

I drove Michelle to the Westin Hotel. I was informed there were no vacancies. I asked to speak to the manager on duty, took him aside and flashed my phony ID, mentioned something vague about national security and the secured witness program, told him the Justice Department would certainly appreciate the hotel's cooperation. I explained that we were in a serious bind and we'd be truly appreciative if he'd find someplace nice to house this very important young lady for the next few days, I casually mentioned that if we couldn't get cooperation on matters of this sort it might give us reason to reconsider other matters, such as those highly publicized Presidential visits.

Michelle and I were led to a suite on the fifth floor. It boasted a sitting room, bedroom and a bath. I wrote my burner number and Miles' number as a secondary contact, told her we'd check in several times a day to make sure she was all right, and to call us if she needed anything. No, she shouldn't go outside, and no, she shouldn't tell anyone where she was staying. I promised to get some cash to her the next morning.

I climbed into the Mercury and drove toward Pioneer Square, found a space in a lot near Union Street, and walked back to Fifth Avenue. I perched just around the corner on Virginia, out of sight, but with a clear view of the Westin's entrance. It was almost an hour before Pear stepped out of a cab and entered the lobby.

FROST

Chapter Twenty-Four

I'd recorded my Hal Jordan alias on the registry for Michelle's room. I stopped at the desk and got a keycard, took the elevator to the fifth floor.

I palmed the Ruger. I heard voices talking inside the room, Pear's and Michelle's, both calm, subdued. I slipped the keycard into the slot as quietly as I could and when the light flickered green I turned the doorknob.

Pear sat in a brown leather armchair. "Hello, Micah." He slowly lifted his arm, waved an automatic pistol in my direction. "Can I get you a drink? Michelle, please fetch my brother a bourbon and water. I hope that will suffice, the bar is woefully understocked. If I were paying for this room what you're paying for this room, I'd complain to the management."

My own gun pointed toward Pear's chest. "I'm more concerned about the vermin problem."

"Please don't talk about Michelle that way. She's young and impressionable and we don't want to hurt her feelings."

"That would perhaps explain her lack of taste in men."

"Have you spoken to Dad lately?"

"Fuck you."

"Ah, that's right. We don't speak of our parent."

Michelle brought me the drink. "You lied to me," she said.

"Not nearly as much as you think."

"Can we put these things away?" Pear asked. "I doubt we'll actually shoot each other, the noise would disturb the other guests. Michelle, please get me a drink, my usual. And get one for yourself." Pear lifted forward, slid the handgun into a holster above his right hip. "Is there some reason you went to so much trouble to talk to me?"

"I'm looking for a girl."

"Aren't we all?"

"This one is fifteen years old, spent some time locked up in that house of yours on Halleck."

"This would be the same number supposedly pregnant by Wainwright."

"Still perceptive, I see."

"I don't know where she is." Pear took a long pull on his drink, handed the empty glass to Michelle. "Another, please darlin'."

"You have no idea where the girl is?"

"I wish I did. You wouldn't know anything about a few flashdrives I'm missing?"

"You really should have an alarm on that house of yours."

"I do. Somebody disabled it without my consent."

"I want the girl."

"Let's suppose that maybe I can help. What's in it for me?"

"A half-dozen pornographic flashdrives, maybe. Maybe even another couple with banking information on them."

"Your negotiating skills have improved considerably."

"The stuff on those drives is only useful to you as long as it's confidential information. If it becomes public--"

"Point noted."

"If the girl isn't returned unharmed in twenty-four hours, my associates guarantee that every television network, major news organization and sleazy Internet operation gets copies of everything we've got."

FROST

Pear tongued an ice cube from the tumbler, rolled it around inside his mouth. He pursed his lips, smiled at Michelle, turned back to me. "I'll see what I can do."

"One more thing, Pear: who killed Camey Horne?"

"Damned if I know. I had an idea, but the three idiots I had in mind turned up dead. That doesn't mean they didn't do it, but it does make it harder to beat a confession out of them."

"They were flunkies. I want to know who ordered it."

"So do I." Pear sat his drink on the coffee table. "And when we find out who did it, Micah, whoever it is, is mine."

"Sentimental much?"

"Nobody fucks with me, Micah, not for long. You'd do well to remember that."

I looked at Michelle. "He certainly is a charmer. Are you staying with him?"

Michelle looked from me to Pear, back to me. "For now."

I shook my head and left the hotel room, rode the elevator to the lobby, checked out and settled the bill.

FROST

Chapter Twenty-Five

We sat in the Americana. Donna said she wasn't hungry and so did Miles. I ordered breakfast for them anyway.

The Sunday morning Broadway crowd filtered in, boys in denim jeans and leather jackets, girls in black skirts and camouflage trousers. The occasional tourist stumbled through, tie wrapped securely around a starched white collar, wife wrapped securely around a white arm, both nonplussed at the number of same sex couples out for an early weekend meal.

The waitress brought food, and lots of it. I outlined my plan to Donna and Miles while we ate. Neither was much impressed by my partnering with Pear, nor were they convinced I should trust him.

I told them I didn't.

I needed Pear to find Wainwright. I was betting Wainwright would want to make certain he had the right girl, so Serena would have been brought to him rather than eliminated. The photo prints I'd given Wainwright were fuzzy at best, it wouldn't do to kidnap the wrong victim, and Wainwright would want to confirm that Serena was indeed pregnant with his child.

I figured Wainwright would have been someplace last night where he would have been seen by a large number of his supporters, especially after the confrontation with Donna, and I didn't think he'd be stupid enough to take Serena into his own home, what with the police and Mrs. Wainwright unlikely to commiserate with his circumstance. I hoped for some down time until Wainwright could rendezvous with the hired help and verify

FROST

Serena's condition--a condition unfortunately easily verified with an inexpensive over-the-counter ice cream stick one need only to pee on.

My phone rang. I glanced at the display, noted the number of the burner Pear carried. It was time.

Miles hugged me, wished me luck, then Donna, a little too long and a little too tight.

I laid a hundred dollar bill on the table and walked out of the restaurant, got into the Mercury and pulled away. I'd died once this week and I hoped I wasn't driving into a repeat performance.

FROST

Chapter Twenty-Six

"Wainwright is at a cabin he owns outside Greenwater," Pear said.

"Where's Greenwater?"

"Other side of Enumclaw, toward Mr. Rainier. It's one of those hunting lodge kind of places. He'll have two goons with him, and both of them are good. One is Ray Sturgill, Wiley to his friends. He's an ex-Navy Seal, ex-DOD spook. The other is a guy named Robert Long. Robbie spent a few years with Wiley at DOD. They actually worked for the old man for a couple of years. Both were rolled out for Unsatisfactory Performance, and you can read that as a psych issue. "

I could see Pear's eyes glisten.

"Wainwright always keep that kind of firepower on his payroll?"

"Keeps away guys like you and me, and believe me, there are more of us than you might think. Wainwright hand-picked these two misfits."

"How do you know so much about them?"

"We used to be a trio." Pear slapped a clip into the butt of a Walther PPQ 9mm and dropped the gun into a soft leather shoulder holster. "It's amazing what kind of stuff gets thrown at a guy in Wainwright's position. Everybody wants something, you know? Company A wants this defense contract, Company B wants a special exemption of import or export duties, Company C wants access to sensitive foreign intelligence in order to better forecast their overseas operations. They shovel money at him by the truckloads. And women, of course, and property.

"Wainwright has to be insulated, so they go through Wiley and Robbie. And me, up until I went out on my own. We'd bury the assets through a series of dummy corporations, mostly consulting companies.

"Got too big, though, too quick. Somebody had to set something up and run it like a business. Wiley and Robbie didn't have the taste for that, so I got elected."

"I'm happy for you."

"Over time, I managed to move a substantial portion of those assets into companies bearing only my name."

"Wainwright allowed this?"

"Wainwright found out after the fact. I offered him a cut, which is safer for him, anyway. I make deposits to him down in the Caymans."

"Maybe he wants it all back."

"Wainwright likes little girls, and he knows what happens to his whole damn life if it becomes public knowledge. He gets his cut, it can't be traced to him, and everybody wins."

"Everybody except the kids."

Pear looked at me dully. "Kids my ass. These kids, as you call them, grew up on the street and they grow up pretty quick out there. They'd made the decision to run away from whatever they were running away from and they've all sold themselves many, many times before they ever come to us. Once they're with us nobody is punching on them, they're housed and fed and warmed and clothed. It's a much better deal for them than the street."

"And they can leave anytime they want."

"Pretty much."

FROST

"Serena tells a different story."

"The pregnant girl? I'm sure she does. Why are you so hot to get her back, anyway? I wouldn't have thought she'd be your type."

I almost killed Pear, right then and there, but I thought better of it. I didn't know the exact location of Wainwright's retreat and I didn't even know if the place was in his name. Instead, I made a mental promise that when this was all over I'd wipe Pear off the face of the Earth.

"We keep this simple," Pear said, "we drive toward Greenwater, stop for lunch, pull into Wainwright's cabin, take out Wiley and Robbie, then, assuming she's there, grab the girl and go."

"What about Wainwright?"

"I'll handle Wainwright."

"Going to kill him, just like your other two ex-partners?"

"Depends. If he had Camey done, probably. If he didn't, maybe not."

I shook my head. "I just want the girl."

"You're beginning to sound like a broken record. Remember records?"

"Only thing I can remember at the moment is that same old tune."

Pear's eyes rolled back in his head. "Whatever."

***

Pear gunned the BMW. We passed Renton and Maple Valley, roared through Black Diamond and into Enumclaw, a sleepy little burg filled with 1920s semi-Victorian houses and a

FROST

wide denominational variety of churches. I counted thirteen of them along the main drag, knew there would be more buried inside the tiny village.

Pear hadn't been joking about lunch. He pulled into the parking lot of a highway diner and parked the car. "I miss grits," he said after we'd slid into opposite sides of a back booth and placed our orders. "And those small fried catfish. You can't get 'em here or in L.A. Camey and I caught a flight to Atlanta once, told the cabbie to take us to a good seafood restaurant. I ate catfish and grits for almost two hours, and then we caught a flight back to Los Angeles."

"Camey was big on southern fried seafood?"

"Hell, no. Camey was big on profit and loss. She spent the whole flight punching a laptop. That was okay, though. Damn, that girl could hide cash assets. I hold the papers on half-a-dozen non-profits that only accept corporate donations. It's a trick to run money through them and out of the country without arousing the IRS, but that girl was genius at it."

"Nine billion dollars a year genius?"?

"Somewhere around that. You reach a point where you stop counting."

"If you're doing that well, why bother with pimping kids?"

The waitress brought a cup of coffee and two frosty beer bottles. I took the coffee. Pear pulled both bottles toward him, then rubbed at the lip of the first bottle. "It helps to have a way to clear through some of the clutter for export of certain commodities, say, computers or medical supplies. Or weapons.

"Wainwright always liked little girls, at least from the time I met him. I sort of acquired the staff of a D.C. pimp ten years ago, unknown to the Senator, of course. Simple matter to tape the activity, and by the time Wainwright figured out I was taking over, I literally had him by the balls. Besides, he knew I was trustworthy, after a fashion. He gets his jollies, I get government help moving my clients' goods around the world on military transport at no cost and no tariffs.

"It's a funny thing, though. Remember that kid back in Carolina, the gay boy we met when we were, what, thirteen or fourteen? Seemed like he knew every gay person in a three state area. These guys are just like he was. They all seem to know each other.

"So Wainwright starts a sort of gift service for those people he knows who are of a like mind. I taped them, and suddenly Wainwright's got an incredibly enthusiastic long line of wealthy financial contributors for his next campaign."

"And every campaign after that. How does Steven Cook fit into this?"

"I met Cook when he was in college. Initially, he was my video guy and later, after he graduated, he'd go to work at media outlets StoneVentures had an interest in acquiring and feed me inside information."

"Sweet guy."

"He's an idiot, but he's good with a camera."

"Five-by-sevens?"

Pear took a long pull at his beer. "Interesting thought."

The waitress brought two serving platters. Each held a chunk of charbroiled beef covered with thick unpeeled fried potatoes. Pear ordered more beer and asked for steak sauce.

"Tell me," Pear said, cutting into his steak, "why'd you decide to kill yourself?"

FROST

I watched him shovel a hunk of bloody meat into his mouth. "Self-preservation. Last Saturday night two thugs broke into my home and tried to kill me. Sunday, somebody tucked a handful of plastic explosive into my transmission and almost took my head off."

"Why not just take them out?"

"I wasn't sure who it was. That made it harder to cover myself. I also had some concern for a few people I've gotten close to."

Pear shook his head. "Rule Number Two: Don't get close to anybody. Anyway, now you think it's Wainwright."

"He's my second choice. You were my first."

Pear laid his knife and fork on the side of the platter, took another long pull on the beer bottle. "I do my own work, Micah, always have. I decide you shouldn't be here anymore, I'll show up on your doorstep with a weapon and an explanation."

"I appreciate your directness."

"Have you ever known me to have anyone else do my wet work?"

I remembered London and Madrid, Dublin and the Azores, Detroit and San Francisco. "No," I said. "You generally fought tooth and nail for the privilege of doing your own work."

"Had no choice. You were the one with all the natural talent."

"If I recall, you enthusiasm for the work more than made up for any lack of natural ability."

"If you're being sarcastic, fuck you. If you're not, thanks." Pear chomped another forkful of cow flesh. "So, you drive a rental car off of a bridge--"

FROST

"Micah Frost was a little too hot and too many people were trying to kill him. I needed some breathing room and figured it would be easier to operate without the distractions."

"You really think I did Camey?"

I shook my head. "I don't know who ordered it, but if it had been you it would've been done somewhere other than inside your kitchen."

"I wouldn't have used those three assbrains, either. I would have done it myself."

"Okay."

"You did shake up Cook, by the way. He bought your FBI gag hook, line and sinker."

"Two girl scouts could shake up Cook. He's a real putz."

"And he likes little boys, the younger the better."

"A putz who should be shot. Your choice of companions leaves a lot to be desired, Pear."

"Use all available resources to their best ability, then eliminate when practical."

"I've heard it before, Pear. I didn't like it then, and I don't like it now."

"Your problem is that you've somehow embraced the notion that everybody has the same inherent worth, and that's just plain horseshit."

"No, I didn't buy into that. I just decided that I no longer wanted to be the one responsible for mucking the stable."

We sat for a time, silent. Pear finished his fourth beer while I pushed most of my unfinished steak from one side of its platter to the other and back.

FROST

"Greenwater isn't far," Pear said, finally breaking the silence. "If you remember how to use that broom you don't like to push, we might even make it out of there alive."

FROST

Chapter Twenty-Seven

Pear turned off of the main highway onto what might be described as a dirt trail on those days water didn't pool into blotches of mud along its surface. The drizzle around us precluded dirt. Pear urged the BMW through the muck for almost a mile, and then pulled into a batch of brambles.

"Nice aim."

"Thanks." Pear climbed out of the car and stretched. "Let's get on with it," he said, wiping drizzle away from his beard.

"How far to the cabin?"

"About half-a-mile as the crow flies, 'course you never see any crows in this kind of weather." Pear walked to the back of the car, opened the trunk, and pulled on a pair of leather work gloves. He set to work yanking out stray branches, and then tossed the brambles over the BMW until the automobile was well hidden.

We tramped into the brush, fought thorned vines and slippery wet pine needles. I could smell burning wood, figured we were getting close to the cabin. Another hundred feet brought us to the edge of a clearing.

Log, split and notched, formed a basic triangle. The door and the shutters gleamed fire engine red, the windows between them blinked without curtains. A Jeep parked beside a roughhewn, branch bannistered porch.

Pear slipped the Walther out of its holster and his grin returned. His eyes gleamed like those of a cat who's cornered a live breakfast.

FROST

I grasped the butt of the Ruger, slid the thing out of its harness, and cocked the hammer. I crouched to the ground and edged slowly toward the cabin porch. Pear crab-walked to the opposite corner. We slipped under the bannister and crept to the windows. I ducked under the shutter, raised my head just above the window sill and peeked inside. Wainwright sat alone in the main room facing the fire. I checked from left to right, saw no evidence of anyone's presence.

I looked at Pear. He watched me, grinning all the while. I motioned with my left hand, two fingers down--*all clear*--then two fingers pointed toward the door. Pear nodded. I bobbed my fingers, one, two, three, pounded a fist at the open air, and we charged.

Pear threw his bulk at the heavy door and the doorframe splintered, the door splashed open, and he dove to the floor inside, rolled, gun aimed and ready and I jumped in after him, kissed the floor, somersaulted to my feet and snarled, "Don't move, Wainwright."

Wainwright didn't move. Wainwright didn't respond at all. I gripped the Ruger with both hands, moved around to see Wainwright's face. He stared up at me, eyes glassy, mouth gaping. An uneven crimson star dripped across his chest, pooled into his lap.

I relaxed, dangled the gun at my side.

"Frustrating isn't it?" Pear said. "I'll check upstairs."

Anyone upstairs would certainly have heard our entrance. I rolled my eyes toward Pear, saw the fire behind his pupils. "Whatever."

He reappeared moments later, the Walther nestled back inside its holster. "Nobody here but us Calvary."

FROST

I uncocked the Ruger. "Any sign of Serena?"

"Woodshed's out back," Pear said, motioning me forward. We went out the front door, trudged around to the back of the cabin. A wooden lean-to jutted from the cabin's rear wall. The door sported a padlock clamped through a metal hinge.

"Want me to bust it?" Pear asked.

"Naw." I pulled the Ruger out of the holster, cocked the handgun, and then blasted the lock. The door swung loose, and I pulled it open and stepped inside.

Serena huddled in a corner on the dirt floor. Her raw eyes stared at me in disbelief. I pulled the gag away from her mouth and started to untie her wrists, but Pear tapped me on the shoulder and handed me a notched hunting knife. I sliced the orange plastic rope and lifted the girl to her feet.

Serena's shoulders shook. I hooked my hand around her neck. "Can't I leave you alone for even a minute?"

"We got what we came for," Pear said. Let's go."

The three of us walked to the front of the cabin, headed up the soppy trail toward the car. I saw the Jeep before I heard it, felt the bullet whiz past my ear before I saw the rifle poking through the opened window.

"Shit," Pear grunted. He snatched Serena's arm and leapt into the brush. I dived in after them, hugged the thistle-cluttered muck. Pear looked at me and grinned. "Just like old times."

Pear jumped into a target shooting stance clutching the Walther, his trunk legs spread, knees bent, his gun's barrel shoved toward the oncoming Jeep. He put three slugs through the driver's window as it passed. Shattered glass spewed across the muddy road as the Jeep swerved, slid, skidded into the bush some thirty feet away.

FROST

Pear dropped back into the thorned cover. He reached toward his ankle and grabbed a small automatic pistol. He tossed it at me and I caught it, released the safety and placed the gun into Serena's small hand. "Don't hesitate. They won't."

"I don't know what to do with this," Serena said.

"Just point and pull the trigger," Pear said, "Don't aim. Point and pull, point and pull."

"And don't leave this spot, Serena." The girl nodded, folded her tiny hand around the little pistol, pulled it close to her breast. "Keep your finger outside the trigger guard unless you want to shoot, honey."

Serena nodded again.

"Time to boogie," Pear said. He stepped forward, fought his way through the thick brush.

I jumped across the wet sod trail, rolled into the brambles on the other side, pushed myself up and eased toward the silent Jeep.

The passenger door stood open. I glanced across the way, couldn't see any movement in the brush. I scuffed forward, head low, moved in short spurts until I reached the vehicle. I crouched behind it, peered underneath, found no one hiding there.

I eased around to the open car door, pulled the handkerchief from my back pocket, twisted it, rolled it into a wad. I tossed it into the opening and it fell gracelessly onto the car's seat. I bounced my left hand into the opening and nobody shot at it. I gingerly twisted around and looked into the Jeep.

The car sat empty, bereft of either passenger or driver. Wiley and Robbie were out there waiting, two trained professionals with extraordinary skills and no qualms about

173

FROST

practicing their skills on anyone or anything that came between them and a paycheck.

I glanced back in Serena's direction, couldn't see her, hoped she'd stay down. Wiley and Robbie would probably head for the cabin.

I would've.

I reached the edge of the clearing and looked across the way. I could see Pear's bulk lying flat in the muck, wondered if he could be seen from inside the cabin. Pear found me, pointed, signaled one, two, three, bounced his fat fist against the open air and again we charged the cabin.

I hit the door first, leapt through the opening, rolled to the right, Pear following close behind me. We came to our feet simultaneously, planted ourselves back-to-back, made one complete revolution. The cabin sat empty, save for us and the late Mr. Wainwright.

The phone rang. Pear and I looked at each other, and I reached to the table beside Wainwright and picked up the receiver. "Frost."

"Sturgill. I thought you were dead."

"Not this time."

"There's always tomorrow."

"Is there something you wanted, Wiley? I'm kind of busy right now."

"Robbie and me were wondering if you'd be interested in coming out with your hands up."

"Pear and I were wondering the same thing about you two."

"Hang on, I'll ask." Wiley paused. "I don't mind, but Robbie doesn't trust you."

FROST

"Tell Robbie to go fuck himself."

Another pause, then, "Robbie says if he could do that he'd never leave home."

"Robbie's fucked, anyway. Wainwright's dead and now you two bozos are unemployed."

"Hmmm." Another pause, then, "Ask Stone if he's hiring."

I stared at the receiver for a moment in disbelief, and then tossed it at Pear. "It's for you. I'd check references."

Pear looked at me quizzically, caught the telephone and listened for a moment, then said, "Come on, then. Let's talk." He laid the phone back inside its cradle.

I heard the Jeep's engine in the distance. It fired up, revved, roared in our direction. Wiley and Robbie climbed out of the vehicle, each holding a handgun. They walked to the edge of the porch and waited.

Pear and I gripped our own weapons and stepped outside.

"Didn't mean to shoot at you, Pear," Wiley said. "Didn't realize it was you."

I looked at Pear's bearded bulk, noted the bright red jacket brought to mind an enormous hairy beach ball. "He is hard to recognize."

Robbie kicked at the bottom porch step, knocked a chunk of mud from his shoe. "He works for you, now?"

"Naw. He's my brother."

"No shit?"

"No shit."

"Sorry about the car, Frost. Job, you know? Nothing personal. For what it's worth, I think it was a really cool car."

"Thanks. Was Wainwright also a job?"

"We didn't do Wainwright. We assumed you did."

FROST

"We didn't."

"You get the girl?"

"Yeah."

"Nobody touched her, I promise."

"Good thing."

Robbie tucked his pistol under his arm. "What now?"

Pear followed Robbie's lead, holstered the Walther. Wiley held on to his gun and I held on to the Ruger. "Understand you're looking for work," Pear said.

"If the terms are right."

"I'm sure we can come to terms."

Wiley shoved his handgun into a woven leather pancake mounted on his belt. "Okay, boss, what do you want us to do?"

"Did you kill Camey Horne?" I asked.

Wiley and Robbie looked at Pear. "Answer the man."

"Nope," Wiley said.

"David Welsh?"

"Oh, yeah." Wiley eased a pack of Camel cigarettes from his shirt pocket. "We needed to know where the girl was, and Welsh was less than cooperative." He slipped a packet of matches from under the cellophane wrapping on the pack and struck a match to light his smoke.

"Welsh didn't know where the girl was."

"We didn't know that at the time."

"How'd you find her?"

"Welsh told us you took her. You were dead, but that lady reporter showed up with some pictures you gave her. We followed her, she went to that place on Broadway, and we found the girl."

"Very professional," Pear beamed.

"You get what you pay for."

FROST

"Who told you to bomb my car?"

"Wainwright."

"Okay, guys," Pear said. "Let's get this cleaned up. Lose the Senator, I don't want him found. Ever. Wipe the Jeep and park it at the Airport. Report it stolen."

Wiley laughed. "It is stolen. Anything else?"

"Take a couple of days off. Drop by my offices on Wednesday about noon. We'll talk about your sign-on bonuses. Let's go, Micah."

Pear went down the porch steps and I followed him, finally holstered my gun. We headed toward Serena and the BMW. Once we were out of earshot I asked Pear if he trusted his two new employees.

"Hell, yeah. They are trained professionals with a real love for the work they do and they're completely loyal as long as the check clears. Or, until someone makes them a better offer."

We gathered Serena and I pried the pistol from her fingers. We dug out the BMW, and then drove away from the cabin and Greenwater, headed back to what passes for civilization.

FROST

Chapter Twenty-Eight

Donna guided Serena into the bathroom, helped her with a shower, and then put her to bed.

"I've ID'd the bank accounts," Miles said.

"Any chance I might be able to understand how you did it?"

"Does it matter?"

I shook my head. "Not really. How much are we talking?"

"As nearly as I can figure, around six-and-a-half billion dollars."

"All of it in Stone's name?"

"No, but all of it tied to StoneVentures in one way or another. I'd guess all of his operating money is in those accounts."

"You can manipulate the accounts?"

"Yes." Miles walked to the refrigerator, opened it and removed two Henry Weinhard's, twisted the tops from the bottles, then handed me one of them. "I can do anything the account holder can do, transfer the money to other accounts, close them out." He dropped onto the blue corduroy sofa in the corner.

"Could you be traced?"

"No. Well, maybe. Doubtful. I'd route the directives via sub-servers and then abort the directive data after the transfers were completed, and I'd run a couple of hundred random directive transfers for each account. I wouldn't know how to trace it, and I can't imagine anyone else would be able to."

"How long would it take?"

"All together? About ninety seconds."

FROST

"Okay. Don't move anything, yet, but get everything set up to go."

Miles held the bottle between his legs, fingered the brown glass lip. He stared at the floor, wouldn't look at me.

"Something wrong, Miles?"

"What happened out there?"

"Not as much as you might imagine. Why?"

"Serena's hands are still shaking." Miles took a long pull at the beer. "They took her out of my house, Micah. How is she supposed to sleep here, now? How is she supposed the feel safe? Hell, how am I supposed to feel safe?"

"That's a normal reaction, Miles--"

"Nothing--*nothing*--about this is even close to normal, Micah." Miles pushed himself up off the sofa. I noted the outline of the small Colt I'd given him clearly visible on the right back pocket of his khakis. "Lock the door on your way out."

FROST

Chapter Twenty-Nine

Donna caught me before I reached the car. Her short black hair clung damply to the sides of her head and face and I wondered idly if she'd climbed into the shower with Serena.
"C'mon, I'll buy you a drink."

"I'm not good company right now, Donna."

"What makes you think you're ever good company? Didn't you ever wonder why I have to drink to be near you?"

"I'll try not to make that personal."

"It's important."

I glanced at my watch. It was almost six. Donna took my hand and pulled me toward Vermillion where an Asian boy with bangs greased and plastered against his forehead led us to a wooden booth in the back corner. We slid onto the padded bench seats, Donna on one side and me on the other. Donna ordered two bourbons, neat doubles, and sat quietly until the waiter brought the drinks. "Miles is upset," she said between sips. "He's worried about Serena, but he'll be okay."

"I know."

"What happened out there today?"

"I'll tell you if you promise not to print any of it."

"You know I can't do that."

"Then, I can't talk to you."

"You need to talk to me." Donna propped an elbow on the table, leaned her head into her hand. "Miles is a dear, but he isn't very good about keeping things from me. I know Wainwright kidnapped Serena, or at least had her kidnapped. I know Miles has accessed the accounts on those flashdrives. I know as much about StoneVentures as you do, Micah. Miles showed me everything your researcher dug up, and my own sources pretty much confirm everything he came up with. I also found business connections between Wainwright and Stone, some real estate things worldwide you probably don't even know about, and I know that Stone used to be on Wainwright's staff." She paused. "And I know Stone was a Department of Defense operative assigned to the DIA, as were you."

"Miles doesn't know that."

"I try to be thorough and I have very good sources."

"Wainwright's dead."

"The two thugs who grabbed Serena?"

"They work for Stone, now."

"Did they kill Wainwright?"

"No."

"Did Stone?"

"No."

"Did you?"

"No."

"Do you know who did?"

"No."

"Did you figure out the connection between Shelterville and the rest of Stone's operation?"

"Part of it."

"Have you found Matt's brother?"

"No."

"Do you know who killed Camey Horne?"

"No."

"Do you even know who sent her the pictures?"

I sighed. "No, Donna, I don't."

"Shit."

"Sorry."

Donna pulled another sip from the tumbler. "Well, Wainwright's death will make good copy, at least."

I winced. "You won't be able to prove he's dead."

"What?"

"Wiley and Robbie wiped it. The body will never be found."

"Who are Wiley and Robbie?"

"Stone's newly acquired hired help."

"Oh, fuck."

"Again, sorry."

"At least I've still got your resurrection."

"I need you to hold off--"

"Tomorrow."

"Donna--"

"I'm giving you the chance to comment before the story breaks, Micah."

"I need seventy-two hours."

"Why?"

"To follow up on what I learned today. You wait three days and you've got a much better story with concrete fact to back you up. You go to press tomorrow and you've got little more than half-assed innuendo."

"I've got--I've got--"

"Damned little you can prove, other than the fact that I'm alive and doing well."

FROST

"You're not doing all that well." Donna swirled a finger in the air and signaled for another round. "Seventy-two hours, Frost, no more."

"I think I like you better when you're naked."

"Most men do."

***

Sam Rollins saw me through the glass walls of his office. I walked through the detective pool and knocked on his open door. He didn't get up. "Let me guess," Sam said, "you're the Ghost of Christmas Past."

"Actually, I'm working my way through college and I was wondering if you'd like to buy a subscription to *Crypt & Garden*."

"Close the door."

I did. I dropped into a chair in front of Sam's desk and waited.

Sam looked at me for a long, quiet moment, and then said, "I'm waiting."

"Do you want the version I'll swear to in Court or do you want the truth?

"Give me the Court version."

"I remember driving over the Harbor Island Bridge around midnight. A car came up behind me, fast, ran me off the bridge. I remember going over the rail and hitting the water and the next thing I remember is waking up on the couch in my basement studio."

"And just when did you wake up?"

"A couple of hours ago."

FROST

Sam Rollins might have been Pear's benevolent doppelganger, except that Sam stood about six-foot-one to Pear's five-eight. The grey in Sam's hair and beard, coupled with his jolly grin, often found comparisons to the classic Coca-Cola Santa Claus. He carried his bulk with elegance and authority, and I'd only seen Sam turn ugly on two occasions. The first time, he'd confronted the confessed butcher of half-a-dozen elderly women, and this particular scumbag actually bragged about his exploits, proud of what he'd accomplished. The butcher claimed Sam's aunt as one of his victims.

This was the other time.

"Now tell me the truth."

"Somebody tried to kill me twice in just as many days. I had no idea who the source was and was in no real shape to adequately defend myself after the second attempt. Nobody tries to kill a dead man, so I ran the car off of the bridge and buried myself for a week."

"You mean you took the time to identify and eliminate the source."

"That's not what I said."

"I heard what you said. Now, let me tell you what I've got. I've got a female, one Camey Horne, dead. I've got pictures of the two of you at the scene of the crime with you trying to prod her memory from the wrong end.

"I've got a guy named David Welsh, a guy you asked me to ID from a motorcycle license strung up in his living room. Interestingly enough, turns out he was treated at Harborview a few days before he died for a gunshot wound to the kneecap, a small caliber hand gun the weapon of choice. I've got two dead guys in your bedroom who, Lo and Behold, turn out to be numbers one and two of Welsh's three musketeers, and both dispatched with a small caliber handgun.

"And, if that isn't enough, I've got the Feds digging into Pearson Stone and Senator Jonathan Wainwright, something about influence peddling, racketeering, illegal import and export, interstate prostitution, and possibly operating as agents of a foreign government. You remember Wainwright? He's the one you told me blew up your car. And Stone? The Fibbies got your jacket from DOD, Micah, assuming that's your real name. I wonder since you and Stone are really brothers, but you have different monikers. I checked your record, but it didn't tell me a whole lot, other than your old man was a certifiable maniac and that most everything you did for Uncle Sam is so fucking classified your entire folder can be read in a two-story elevator ride.

"I've got Wainwright on a weekend trip to a cabin in Greenwater, but he's not there and nobody seems to know where he is.

"And now, Casper the Friendly Fucking Ghost strolls into my office and tells me he slept the week away buried in his basement."

"And your point would be?"

"Get yourself an attorney, Micah. Get yourself a good one."

"Am I under arrest?"

"Not yet, but when the Fibbies find out you're alive and kicking you probably will be."

"Are you calling them?"

Sam snorted. "I'm a local yokel. D.C. doesn't sign my paycheck."

"Thanks, Sam."

"I want to think you haven't lied to me, Micah."

FROST

"I also want to think that what you've told me isn't going to come back and bite me in the butt."

"Last I heard it'd cost you fifty bucks to get bit on the butt."

Sam rubbed his eyes. "Get out of my office."

I stood up and headed for the door, but Sam called my name before I could turn the knob. "Yeah?"

"I'm glad you're alive, buddy."

***

I unlocked the door to my room and made a cursory check for hidden assassins. I didn't find any, so I opened the small refrigerator and removed a flask of Jim Beam I'd tucked into it earlier.

On a whim, I pulled out my cellphone and checked my messages. Jeremy Lofgrin told me he was without a doubt the most effective real estate salesperson in West Seattle and he'd be most interested in talking with me about selling my house. I guess he didn't know I didn't own the house.

First Consumers Bank told me I was one of a limited number of people who'd been pre-approved to receive one of their credit cards and all I needed to do was to call back on their toll-free number and they'd arrange to get the card to me.

Peter Sanderson wanted to talk with me about my insurance needs. I thought that was funny, under the circumstances.

Chelsea Holmes told me she'd keep calling until the police could show her a body or until the number was disconnected, whichever came first. She left her new cell number, said she'd keep the damn thing with her at all times. I cleared the cache except for Chelsea's new number, and punched the *Send* button.

"Chelsea," she answered.

"Hi, Sweetheart."

"Are you all right?"

"I'm fine."

"Where are you?"

"The Fairmont."

"What name?"

"Hal Jordan."

"I'll be there in ten minutes."

"Where's Charles?"

"Who fucking cares?"

FROST

Chapter Thirty

Chelsea fell into me and I fell into her.

Crickett fell over both of us, jumped and yipped, her short erect tail quivering as I stroked her head. The dog nuzzled my hand, then trotted off to the bed, leapt onto it and promptly fell asleep.

"I think this is the first time she's slept all week," Chelsea said.

"Would you like a drink?"

Chelsea walked to me, wrapped her arms around me, pressed her blonde head against my chest. "I thought I'd lost you."

I smiled. "Only the good die young. I should be around for decades."

Chelsea looked into my eyes with a depth at once inviting and uncomfortable. I saw a longing in her eyes, a hunger. She pressed her soft lips against mine, kissed me again, probed lightly with her tongue. I felt the room spin, lost all perception of time and space, filled with the scent of her, the soft firmness of pink flesh, the taste of her throat, the touch of her fingertips brushing against my cheek. Suddenly, her hands were all over me and mine all over her, our clothes lost in the frenzy.

Then, it was over.

Chelsea climbed up from the carpet, walked to the refrigerator. She filled two glasses with ice and covered the ice with the Jim Beam in the flask. I'd seen her naked in the photographs, but the pictures lacked the full round sensuality of the woman before me. I watched her move, soaked in the quiet,

FROST

feminine elegance she exuded. She walked back to me, handed me my drink.

"Is there a bed here?" she asked.

I led her across the room, tossed back the bedclothes. Crickett grumbled, moved to a corner at the foot of the bed. Chelsea pushed me down on my back and climbed on top of me.

"You are so very beautiful," I said, my voice thick. Chelsea smiled. She hooked an ice cube with her tongue, leaned over and kissed my stomach, teased my skin with the cold. "Want to see a magic trick?"

"Magic trick?"

"I'm going to raise the dead," she whispered.

***

The sun slid below the horizon hours ago and the autumn clouds joined its escape. The stars in the clear, crisp sky blinked abstractly, winked through the open window at the two of us.

Chelsea curled against me, naked breasts brushing against my chest.

"What happens now?" I asked.

"I want to get on a plane with you. Mexico is wonderful this time of year."

"We can't do that."

"What would you like to do?" I whispered something vaguely obscene. She slid her hand down my belly, gently caressing me. What do you want to do while we're waiting?"

"Waiting?"

"Charles moved out. We talked and he thinks our marriage is just as dead as I think it is. Neither of us is miserable, but we aren't happy, either. And of all things, he's got the hots for a woman who works in his office, another accountant."

"How does Kelly feel about this?"

"Kelly said she love us both, but can't understand why we didn't do this years ago."

"Where is she now?"

"Staying with a friend."

"You were all alone."

"I had Crickett." The dog turned toward us when she heard her name, cocked her head at us. "When she does that it makes her look like she understands what you're saying to her."

"Scary, isn't it?"

"Very. This is, too."

I pushed out of bed and reached for my jeans. "We'll work this all out, but not tonight."

"Are you booting me out?"

I looked at the lovely unclothed woman lying on my bed and couldn't help smiling. "I guess not."

"Good. Bring me some ice."

FROST

Chapter Thirty-One

Steven Cook lived in a condominium on Lake Washington. The balcony afforded a picturesque view of the marina on one side and six lanes of Interstate 5 on the other. It was an easy lock. I slipped inside the place and systematically began my search.

Cook lived like a man with nothing to hide. A peek inside a top desk drawer revealed a handful of magazines not normally available at the local newsstand. I opened the cover of the one on top of the stack and a naked boy peered back at me. I tossed the garbage back into the drawer and closed it.

I found three bankbooks. If the balances were accurate, Cook probably wouldn't worry much if he lost his job.

The nightstand by the bed held a Smith & Wesson .38 Revolver and two companion volumes to the magazines in the living room desk drawer. There were several five-by-seven photographs of undressed boys and each had a name penned on the white border surrounding the color image.

Paul was hand-printed on one of them.

Matt and his brother shared the same hair, the same eyes and chin, and the same cigarette scars.

I walked into the kitchen. Cook's larder indicated a preference for microwaved pre-packaged imitation health food. The refrigerator held four different kinds of fruit juice--none of them a color I'd ever consider putting into my mouth--an unopened gallon of soy milk, a six-pack of O'Doul's near-beer, and two bottles of Canadian Club. I twisted the top off of an O'Doul's and wandered into the laundry room.

FROST

The room opened off of the kitchen. The full-size washer and dryer had been replaced by a piggyback apartment-sized stacking unit. The left half of the nook had been remodeled into a photo printing area. Two obviously expensive digital cameras hung on leather straps in on corner, a Nikon and a Canon, and two wooden shelves held an array of interchangeable lenses, including a telephoto lens that looked powerful enough to watch the man in the moon change his underwear. Two identical Canon color printers stood alongside a stack of glossy photo paper and an old-fashioned X-Acto Paper Cutter.

I opened a file drawer and looked inside. Several hundred manila envelopes perched inside, each holding a single printed photograph and a flashdrive. A numerical code scrawled into the top corner of each envelope, but without some kind of register it would take hours to sort through them and identify something that might tie Cook to Stone. I pulled out a thick handful of the envelopes at random, folded them over and tucked them into my jacket pocket. I'd take a better look at them later.

I stepped back into the kitchen and closed the door to the laundry nook. It was going to be a long day. I tossed the empty bottle under Cook's kitchen sink, headed for the front door, then paused and went back into the bedroom. I reached into the nightstand and grabbed the picture marked *Paul*. I didn't look forward to it, but I'd need Matt to confirm the boy's identity.

I climbed into the Mercury and headed toward downtown. Cook would finish his noon broadcast in twenty minutes and I wanted to know how he'd spend the day.

I picked Cook up as he left the building's main entrance. He drove down Fifth Avenue, parked in a lot and walked to

FROST

Shucker's. I followed from a safe distance, watched him amble into the back as I grabbed a table on the sidewalk.

I could see Cook through the glass, knew he could probably see me, as well, but I hoped that without the geek suit and red glasses he wouldn't notice me. I'd pulled on jeans and a grey wool sweater under a soft suede jacket and hadn't bothered to slick my hair down.

I sipped at coffee, played with a Salmon Salad. I hated Salmon Salad, but I knew it was the one item on the menu the waiter would serve almost immediately.

Cook sat against the back wall, ordered a round of drinks for himself and his guest, folded a menu and placed his order. I pushed the salad to the other side of the table, motioned for the waiter and ordered a steak.

Cook chatted for the better part of an hour. I paid the check and nursed my coffee until his guest got up--I assumed to find the Men's Room--and shuffled into the darkened hallway beyond the back wall. The guest reappeared in a few moments and I recognized Ned Lee, Shelterville's Executive Director.

Cook left ten minutes later. I followed him on foot to Nordstrom's where he picked up a suit he'd apparently bought and left for alterations. Cook puttered through the rest of the afternoon, popped into bookstores and shoe stores and jewelry stores, loitered at quaint little bakeries and pleasant little espresso kiosks, spent too much time wandering through the Pike's Place Market Magic & Novelty Shop. He never did look at the merchandise on the shelves. Shoppers recognized him, trusted him, chatted with him, introduced their children to him. Cook shook the hand of the men, squeezed the shoulders of the women, patted the bottoms of the children shoved at him. I gritted my

FROST

teeth, knew that if I shot him in the toy store I'd never make it out alive.

Cook returned to his car around four-thirty. I followed him back to the television station, watched him head back inside. He'd do the news at five, the update at six-thirty after the national news, and wouldn't leave again until almost eight.

I drove to the corner, turned onto Fifth Avenue and headed toward West Seattle.

FROST

Chapter Thirty-Two

I hadn't been back to the house in West Seattle since my death. Ironically, I was alive, but the house was dead.

Dingy plywood boarded the front windows, an ugly barrier, but effective. The living room hardwood floors showed scars from broken glass and the scuffs of police tromping through. The master bedroom's bed and headboard had been completely destroyed, the dresser mirror shattered, the wooden dresser punctured with a dozen bullet holes. The torn bedroom carpet hosted dried crimson blotches. The interior doors proved useless, hung at odd angles on twisted hinges, their knobs ripped away.

I hustled down the basement stairs. My studio equipment seemed to be in good order. Rapunzel lay across my drawing table, ink stains ruining the image beneath a thin layer of dust. I picked up a draftsman's brush and knocked away the debris wondering when I'd get the chance to rework the piece.

I heard a step behind me, snatched the Ruger from its holster as I spun.

"Put that thing away," Pear said. "If I'd come to kill you, you'd be dead by now."

I dropped the handgun back into its holster. "What do you want, Pear?"

"Why are you following Steven Cook?"

"Just doing my job."

"You don't have a job. A job implies a client."

"I'm the client."

"I want those flashdrives."

FROST

"I might have changed my mind about those."

"I'd hate for Wiley and Robbie to have to go take them from your colleague on Capitol Hill. They're good boys, but they lack a certain finesse."

"Send them after me."

"I've seen you work. I don't want to lose two employees."

"You'd do well to remember that."

"You've seen me work, Micah. You'd do well to remember, as well. Maybe I should just kill you and be done with it."

"Good luck with that."

Pear reached into the breast pocket of his suit jacket and removed a flat gold case. He fingered a thin black cigar and lit it with a cylindrical gold lighter, and then sucked deeply on the cancer stick, held the smoke in his lungs for a moment, then exhaled. "I don't suppose you'd consider working for me?"

"You can't afford me, Pear."

"There are a few things you can't afford, either, Micah. Leave this thing with Camey to me. Back off, for your own good."

FROST

Chapter Thirty-Three

My phone rang. I watched Pear climb into his BMW as I answered. "Frost."

"Micah? Sam Rollins. The Federal boys are with me and they aren't real happy about your second coming. They want to talk. Do you want to come in or do you want us to come to you?"

I wasn't about to invite Fibbies into my house unless they'd secured a warrant. "I'll come to your office."

"Half-an-hour, buddy, otherwise you're the bottom end of an APB."

"Gotcha."

"I mean it, Micah."

***

"Micah, Agents Harmon and Steadley, FBI." Harmon and Steadley both wore the same sad blue suit I'd gratefully dropped into a Goodwill bin. Sam nodded to an empty seat and I claimed it.

"I assume you're armed," Harmon said.

"I am."

"Would you mind removing your weapon." It wasn't a question.

"Am I under arrest?"

"No."

"I'm carrying legally, and yes, I'd mind very much."

FROST

Steadley removed his jacket and loosened his tie. "There are two ways we can do this, tough guy."

"Please stop flexing all those muscles. I frighten easily."

"Listen, smartass, you are this close--" Steadley held up his thumb and index finger, an inch of space between them.

"That's good." I lifted my own hand, all fingers folded except the erect middle one. "Can you do this?"

"I don't think you understand the trouble you're in, Mr. Frost." This was Harmon.

"I'm not in any trouble. If you had anything on me, you'd have locked me away by now. You want to talk, talk--otherwise I'm out of here. By the way, if you insist on this good-cop-bad-cop crap you should really study a Dirty Harry movie and learn how to do it properly."

We all sat for a moment. Nobody spoke. I stood up.

"Where do you think you're going?" Harmon asked.

"I figured you'd lost your voice." I thought I saw Sam Rollins smile a little, but I could've been wrong.

Harmon laid a steel attaché case on Sam's desk and opened it. He pulled out a handful of manila folders. "Do you know a Jonathan Wainwright?"

"Not personally."

"He's missing."

"My joy knows no bounds."

"Do you know where he is?"

"No."

"You were seen having a drink with him at the Pike's Place Bar & Grill a while ago. What were you talking about?"

"The perceived basic ineptitude of the average Justice Department employee."

FROST

"Cute."

"Thanks."

"And you insist you don't know where he is?"

"Who?"

Harmon gritted his teeth. "Wainwright."

"Jonathan?"

Steadley slammed his fist against the desktop. "You are looking at an Obstruction of Justice--"

"That was better," I said. "Lots of emotion in that one."

"Do you know a Pearson Stone?"

"Can one person ever really know another?"

Harmon opened one of the folders. "Says here he's your twin brother."

"You're wasting my time, Harmon, and I've enjoyed just about as much of this as I'm going to put up with."

"You want to tell us about your work with DOD?"

"No."

"Are you still classed active?"

"What does the file tell you?"

"The file tells me that information is classified."

"You're beginning to bore me, big time."

"Do you know Camey Horne?"

"I did."

"In the Biblical sense?"

"Steadley is the bad cop, remember?"

"Did you know she was working for us?"

"Did she know she was working for you?"

"Wainwright has been under investigation for the past year. Influence peddling, misuse of power, and racketeering. He's tied to StoneVentures through your brother. Miss Horne contacted us initially, made us aware of some confidential information--"

"What information?"

"It's confidential," Steadley snarled.

"And they trust you with it?"

"We think maybe Wainwright found out about the investigation and decided to visit a friendlier climate," Harmon said. "What do you think?"

"I think I'd like to know who killed Camey Horne."

"That is a local matter. Ms. Horne was not a Federal employee, exactly, and we're not involved in that aspect of this."

I stood up. "We're done here."

"We'll probably want to speak with you again."

"You can reach me through my attorney. His number is in the book."

"What's his name?"

"That's in the book, too."

FROST

Chapter Thirty-Four

I left Sam Rollins' office and drove up Aurora Avenue, pulled off on Phinney Ridge and stopped at Shelterville.

Ned Lee wasn't in. No, the female scarecrow on duty wasn't authorized to give me his home address. No, she wasn't able to call him at home and let me speak to him. I didn't have his number because he'd conveniently forgotten to include his own personnel folder in the information he'd given me earlier.

I drove idly, found myself back on Aurora Avenue headed north. I remembered the envelopes I'd pilfered from Cook's condominium and decided to take a better look at them.

I pulled into the Burgermaster Drive-In and flipped on my headlights. A young girl with red hair leaned into the Mercury's window. She'd apparently practiced the angle of entry for quite some time, twisted to a perfect degree that allowed her tight, white blouse to gape open. She'd left the top clasp unsnapped and I found myself gazing through two soft mounds of mammary tissue to her navel. She wore an innie.

"Great car," she said. "I just love red seats."

"Matches your bra."

The girl blushed so quickly I wondered if that might also be a practiced gesture. "I'm Randy," she said.

"I can tell."

"What can I get for you?"

"A club sandwich and a large black coffee."

Randy licked her upper lip. "Anything else?"

"Not until I regain some strength."

FROST

Randy waltzed toward the kitchen. I watched her spandex wrapped butt swing back and forth, and smiled. There was a time I'd have been flattered, but that was before I'd come to the realization that this stretch of Aurora Avenue boasted the heaviest concentration of hookers in the greater Seattle area. Chances were that Randy wasn't enchanted by my inherent charm and good looks, but was in a roundabout way looking for a quick part-time gig.

I reached into the glove compartment and retrieved the envelopes. Most of what Cook had filed away were simply scenic shots, a lot of seascapes, and it turned out that Cook was quite good. I'd gone through four of the envelopes by the time Randy returned with my sandwich. I thanked her, dismissed her in as polite a manner as I knew how, and unwrapped the foil around the food.

If Camey Horne fed information to the FBI, why would she have asked me for help leaving Pear? It made no sense. And who killed her? Pear wasn't a likely candidate under the circumstances. I hadn't been able to tie Wainwright to her, so I was inclined to believe Wiley and Robbie's claim of innocence. David Welsh's cohort had confessed to the killing, but hadn't offered information on who'd ordered it, and it wasn't as if Blondie, Bozo and Dick Dastardly were sharp enough to put together some kind of takeover.

Takeover.

Pear'd told me Camey wanted a good-sized chunk of his operation, felt she'd earned it. Could she have found a way to absorb the legal operational aspects of StoneVentures, provided Pear was out of the way? It was certainly possible and could explain why she'd slipped information to the Fibbies, but it didn't explain why she was dead and who'd killed her. It didn't explain who'd sent photo prints of her coupled with Pear or who'd sent pictures of Chelsea and Camey to me. It didn't explain who'd order the first attempt on my life. I knew Wainwright had ordered the bomb in my car, but if he'd been the one who ordered the home invasion Wiley and Robbie would've shown up instead of the Clown Twins.

Not to mention, I'd probably be dead and completely unconcerned about any of this.

My head hurt. I tossed the greasy sandwich back on the window tray and picked up another envelope. Camey Horne had been a beautiful woman, secure in her appearance, proud of her image. She'd been the kind of woman who'd use her looks and her body to help accomplish whatever end she found appealing. And, she was brilliant.

Camey's beauty filled the proof sheet in my hand. There were some thirty photos, each an image of the late Camey Horne. The first were simple portraits, but as the frames progressed Camey lost her clothing and demonstrated an extraordinary gymnastic ability at stretching and twisting. A number of the shots were beautiful, gallery quality images of a lovely undraped woman suitable for hanging in almost any setting, but there were a fair number of the kind of images that routinely result in zoning lawsuits brought against Adult Entertainment Centers by the other residents in the vicinity.

Cook worked with Pear from StoneVentures inception and might know where a lot of buried bodies were hidden. If Camey wanted to take over Pear's company, she most certainly would have been astute enough to identify those things that would have endeared her to whatever hired help might have been useful. Sex with Cook was out of the question because of his twisted preferences, but photography was his avocation and she could offer him a confidential subject for his lenses he might have difficulty matching through his own efforts. The sessions would have allowed the two of them to talk, become close, begin to wonder aloud how it might be to their mutual benefit to join forces and ease out Pear.

I set the proof aside, perused the others. I found two more proofs with Camey as the subject. Another featured Chelsea Holmes, the four shots delivered to me and thirty-two others. Fourteen documented various stages of undress in preparation for a shower; six others demonstrated the proper manner to towel dry after emerging from a cascade of steaming water. I tucked the rest of the envelopes back into the glove compartment, folded the proofs of Camey and Chelsea and stuck them into my jacket pocket. It was time to have another chat with Steven Cook.

I flipped on my lights, gave Randy a twenty for an eight dollar meal. She thanked me, tossed a telephone number instead of my change. I started to say something, then realized she was getting by probably the only way she knew how, not much different from the rest of us and at least she was honest about it.

"How old are you, Randy?" I asked as she unhooked the serving tray from my window.

"Old enough," she said.

"Aren't we all?"

FROST

Chapter Thirty-Five

Cook unlocked his front door and tossed his sport coat on the floor. He closed the door and clipped on the safety chain, then loosened his tie and kicked off his shoes.

"Welcome home," I said.

I sat in the corner perched on a leather ottoman. Cook glared in my direction and then walked toward the desk. "Jordan? Or should I call you Frost?"

"Which do you prefer?"

"I prefer shithead."

"Clever, for a dead man."

Cook glanced over his shoulder at me and snorted. "Yeah, right. I'm going to have a drink. Want one?"

I held up half a bottle of O'Doul's.

"Glad to see you're making yourself at home." Cook ambled to the refrigerator, retrieved a bottle of Canadian Club. He poured a stiff measure of booze, dropped in two ice cubes and drifted toward the sofa, a tumbler in one hand and the bottle in the other. "You're trespassing," he said. "What's the penalty for breaking and entering, anyway? Or for impersonating a Federal Officer?"

"Don't know, offhand. I do know the penalty for murder."

Cook guzzled half the tumbler. "No penalty as long as you don't get caught."

"Got it all figured out, right?"

"I'll get there, I've got time."

"You're out of time."

"Don't threaten me, you little punkass."

"Punkass." I pushed myself up from the ottoman and walked to the sofa and poured the remaining beer onto Cook's crotch. He started up at me and I pressed the empty bottle against his trachea. "Please do."

Cook slunk back into his seat.

"You take nice pictures," I said. "Tell me about the ones you sent to Camey."

"What are you talking about?"

I slammed the bottle into his throat. Cook gagged, gasped for air, choked again. I hoped he didn't vomit. "I found the proofs in your laundry room."

The color slowly seeped back into Cook's cheeks. "So what?"

"I found some other things, too, things I find upsetting." I pushed my face into his. "I'm going to ask and you're going to answer, and you'd better answer quickly and completely, otherwise I'm going to become even more upset. If that happens, I'm going to do things to you with this beer bottle that you will remember in absolute terror every moment for the rest of your very short life."

Cook's eyes looked into mine, wavered, and then closed.

"Pictures," I said.

"Camey had me take the pictures."

"I'm waiting."

"Could you please move the bottle?"

"No."

Cook exhaled and the redness in his cheeks became sallow. "Camey sent the pictures to herself, spoofed an email account and put your name on it, then printed the thing."

"Why?"

"I want to call my lawyer."

"Tough. I'm not a cop."

Cook sighed. "She figured if Pear thought you were after them, he'd kill you. Or you'd kill him defending yourself. Either way, Pear's out of the picture."

"Pear would've been out of the picture if Camey had just given his account ledger to the FBI."

"Pear has viable, legitimate business operations, things that grew out of the other stuff. It would take years for the government people to sort through what's what, and there was no guarantee that even the legit part would come back to Camey. She was transferring the legal assets into our names, but she was afraid Pear was suspicious, and Pear suspicious is a very dangerous situation. Your brother is not a nice man."

"How'd you know we were brothers?"

"Camey told me."

"How'd she know?"

"I have no idea."

I pulled the bottle away from Cook's throat and stepped back. "Shelterville."

"Lee recruits kids off the streets, picks what he considers the top of the lot and puts them into houses."

"I was told Stone has places in most every major city in the world."

"So I'm told."

I pulled Paul's photograph out of my pocket, threw it at Cook. "Where is this one?"

Cook's eyes filled with tears. "Tokyo, I think. Pear sent him there."

FROST

"Why?"

Cook wiped his eyes on the back of his hand. "I don't know."

"I am still prepared to feed you this bottle," I said matter of factly.

"I loved him," Cook whispered.

"Meaning what?"

"I wouldn't let Pear put Paul into the system. Paul was a beautiful boy. I wanted him for my own."

"But Pear thought that was dangerous."

"There are ways. We could've pretended he was my son."

I backhanded him. Cook's face snapped toward his right shoulder, blood flung from his nostrils. "How do we get him back?"

"He's either sold or dead."

"Sold?"

"There's a market for everything, Frost."

"Who killed Camey?"

"I don't know."

"I don't believe you."

"Then kill me and get it over with. You're going to do it, anyway."

"Who killed Wainwright?"

"I don't know that, either."

"Wouldn't happen to know who sent the two idiots to my house in the middle of the night?"

Cook shook his head. "You spilled my drink."

I shook my head, waved him toward the kitchen. "Go."

Cook refilled his glass and sat down on a barstool across the room.

FROST

"What were you and Ned Lee talking about?"

"Lee wants more money."

"For what?"

"He gets a five thousand dollar bonus for each acceptable unit and he doesn't think it's enough."

"Unit. What'd you tell him?"

"I told him to talk to Pear."

"That should be an interesting conversation. What exactly did Camey transfer into your names?"

"I don't know. She died before she could tell me."

I laughed, couldn't help it. "A chunk of a multi-billion dollar business is sitting somewhere with your name on it, but you don't know how much, where it is and don't have the slightest idea of how to find out."

Cook nodded. "Pretty much."

I laughed again. "You know Pear will find out. He's very thorough."

"I know."

"What are you going to do?"

"What are you going to do to me?"

"Nothing," I said. "Not a damned thing." I walked to the front door and out of the condominium wondering just how many newscasts Cook had left.

***

Wiley and Robbie were waiting at my car. "We've done this before," I said.

Wiley grinned. "You're not on our list today, Frost."

FROST

"That's something, I guess. I thought you boys were on vacation."

"Slight delay," Wiley said. "Pear uncovered a few financial discrepancies he needed explained."

"You boys don't strike me as accounting types."

"We just translate," Robbie said.

I nodded.

"Look, Frost, I've got nothing against you. Frankly, as near as I can tell you're just like us." Wiley paused, glanced at Robbie, then back at me. "I think Robbie kind of likes you, too."

"I'm flattered."

"Stone told you to stay out of this."

"What's your point, Wiley?"

"I don't want you, Frost. There are too few of us guys around for us to be jumping at each other, but if Stone tells me to jump, well, that's my job."

"Not going to be an easy workday if that happens, Wiley."

"I appreciate that. I'd still have to give it my best shot."

"I respect that, Wiley. I'll miss having you around."

"Cook upstairs?"

I glanced back at the condominium. "Yeah."

"We have to have a little chat with him. You finished or do you need him later?"

I shook my head. "I don't need him. I don't think anybody needs him."

"That was the word we got," Wiley said. "Oh, and before I forget, Ned Lee won't be any help to you. He died in an automobile accident. His brakes went out and he shot off that hill coming down Phinney Ridge."

"When did that happen?"

FROST

Robbie looked at his watch. "Assuming he leaves work on time, about three minutes from now."

FROST

Chapter Thirty-Six

I felt foolish standing outside Miles' door with a handful of fresh cut flowers, but here I was. I knocked and knocked again. Miles opened the door and looked into what I hoped was a solemn, sincere expression on my face. I could see him fight for control, but he snickered, then giggled, then laughed aloud, long and hard, and I knew everything would be okay.

"Don't just stand there, looking like some nervous suitor." Miles took a deep breath and blew it out between clenched teeth. "You do know you're not my type?"

"Fuck you."

"Not a chance, hotshot, not a chance."

Miles pulled me inside, hugged me awkwardly with one arm. "Very pretty. Who helped you?"

I pretended to scowl. "You think I can't pick out flowers on my own?"

"So, what, one of the girls at QFC? Not the little blonde girl?"

"Not unless she's dyed her hair jet black since the last time you saw her."

"Sit," Miles said, waved at the couch. "Would you like a beer?"

"I'd like a '56 Monterey, but I'll settle for a beer."

Miles laid the flowers on the dining table, opened the small refrigerator by the computer desk and pulled out a Michelob. He tossed it across the room and I caught it, twisted the top slowly to allow some of the shaken carbonation to escape. I lifted the bottle into the air. "To good friends."

Miles pointed his own in my direction. "To real friends."

"Where's Serena?"

"Shopping. For school."

"Oh, ho. What's the deal?"

"I took her over to Central this morning and got her and Matt tested. Matt's about where I thought he'd be, but Serena--" Miles beamed like a proud father "--Serena tested out at a second year college level."

"You're sending her to college?"

"Yes, we are."

"We?"

"I thought maybe she could attend on the Pearson Stone Scholarship Fund."

"I like it. Does she know where she wants to go?"

"The University of Washington, Seattle campus."

"How do we get her enrolled?"

"I enrolled her about an hour ago."

"Really."

"I put her in the UW computer as a transfer student from the University of Virginia."

"Transcripts?"

"Neatly acquired and filed."

"Is she living on campus?"

"She'll live here until she's had a chance to adjust, make some friends and settle into a routine. At that point, we'll see about getting her an apartment of her own. By the way, she'll need a car."

"Does she have a Driver's License?"

"She will have just as soon as the DMV sends her the replacement copy."

"She had a license before?"

"No. We have to teach her to drive."

"Did you pay her tuition yet?"

"Haven't touched any of that money, not until you say so."

I nodded. "What about Matt?"

"Matt tests average for a nine-year-old, but he's a little behind because he's missed a lot of school. We can get him privately tutored to bring him up to speed, but that's not the real problem."

Miles tugged at an ear. I hoped he wouldn't rip the earring through the lobe. "People are going to be looking for him, Micah. He's got parents somewhere and they may have filed a police report. I could phony something up, but there's always the chance of it blowing up in our faces and leaving Matt flapping in the breeze."

"Nobody's looking for the girl?"

"Serena came up from California after her mom died. Stepdad's a Neanderthal with a twisted concept of what a relationship with a stepdaughter is supposed to be. I took her down to Social Security with a Birth Certificate I put together and told them I was her father. They gave her a card and bingo, instant ID, new identity."

"New last name?"

"Stemper. Serena Stemper."

"Miles, your image is shot all to hell."

Miles grinned. "Thought it might expand my horizons. I can join Parents Without Partners."

FROST

"I could get you one of those bumper stickers, you know, *My kid is an Honor Student at the University of Washington*."

"I could eventually become a grandfather."

"Assuming you let Serena date somebody other than your friends."

"Oh, shit, I hadn't thought about that."

"Miles, Miles, Miles."

"Anyway, back to Matt. I've taken the liberty of preparing a custody release," he said. He reached into a drawer and pulled out a legal-looking paper, complete with blue cardstock cover. "This effectively transfers permanent custody to Donna."

"With her schedule? She's never home."

"Matt will spend ten months of the year in boarding school. It's not a perfect solution, but it keeps him safe, gets him an education and gives him a shot at a good life."

"Same scholarship fund, I take it?"

"Stone is a very generous man."

I glanced at the form in my hand. "Is this really legal?"

"I have a law degree, Micah, and I'm admitted to the Bar to practice in the states of Washington, Oregon and California."

"I did not know that. So it's legal?"

"It will be once Matt's custodial parent signs it."

***

I drove out toward Federal Way, a grungy little piece of habitation south of Seattle and north of Tacoma. The main drag, Pacific Highway South, filled with run down taverns, mobile home sales lots, used car emporiums and strip joints.

FROST

Matt's family lived two blocks behind a tavern called the *Dew Drop Inn*. I swear, that's what the tattered neon sign flickered.

I parked the Mercury and climbed out. Remnants of abandoned automobiles filled the yard. Engine blocks lay at odd angles among pieces of fender and rusted-out exhausts. Ruined tires piled across the sidewalk. I stepped around the pile into uncut weeds, fought my way to the front door and knocked.

A beefy young man answered the door. "Whaddya want?"

"Are you John Dakker?"

"Who wants to know?" He turned his head at an angle, squinted one eye. He had Matt's curly red hair, but he'd neglected to cut it for a year or so and it hung in uneven clumps around his bullet-shaped head.

"My name's Frost. I need to talk with you about your sons."

"Those fuckin' brats?" Dakker pulled the door toward him, but I pushed my hand inside and grabbed his arm.

"Dakker, I am going to talk with you one way or another. Do you want to do this inside or out here in this junkyard?"

"John?"

"Shut up, Myra."

I grabbed Dakker at the snap of his jeans and yanked. He tumbled through the door and skidded onto the sidewalk. He cursed, scrambled to his feet, pulled himself to his full height. He was a good head taller than me, maybe a hundred pounds heavier. Dakker curled a fist the size of my head and threw it at my jaw. I stepped inside the punch, slapped his cheek. I crammed my elbow into the soft spot just beneath the center of his ribs, jerked the

FROST

back of my closed hand against his nose. Blood spurted across his naked chest.

"Had enough?" I asked.

The son-of-a-bitch kicked at me. I stepped back, watched him drop into a Kung Fu stance that could only have come from late night television reruns. Dakker spun. I pushed my open hand against his heel and pushed, and he landed on his butt. He scurried to his feet, but I'd had enough. I planted my left boot firmly on the concrete sidewalk, bent, drove my right boot into his abdomen, pulled back, spun, and slammed it into his left cheek. Dakker's eyes rolled back into his head and he melted into the unmowed grass.

I hooked Dakker at the middle of his waistband and drug him inside. A nervous little woman with a sallow complexion and runny eyes peered at me from across the room. "Hello, Myra," I said.

"Who are you?"

"I'm a friend of Matt's. Are you his mother?"

"I'm with John. Matt's his boy, not mine."

"Where's his mother?"

"Run off a couple of years ago."

"How come?"

The woman looked at the man piled on the floor. "John gets, well, he's got a temper sometimes. When he drinks." Myra looked up at me. "He's really a good man, though."

"What brand does he smoke?"

"Cigarettes? Carlton."

"Get me a pack, would you please, Myra? And some matches. Thank you." The woman shuffled off, returned with the smokes. "Myra, do you have a telephone in your bedroom?"

FROST

"Phone's in the kitchen."

"Okay. Myra, do you want to stay with this--with John?"

"Of course I want to stay with John."

"Go into your bedroom and shut the door. Turn on the radio, loud. Don't come out, no matter what you hear, understand?"

"No, I don't understand."

"I have to talk with John about his sons, Myra. The older boy, Paul, is dead."

"My god."

"It might be better if you weren't here in the room."

"John's gonna be pissed."

"Go into the bedroom, Myra."

I lit two cigarettes, placed them in the ashtray. Dakker had most of a Rhinelander sitting in front of him, and I picked up the can and poured it over his head. The foamy slime covered his eyes, bubbled into his gaping mouth. Dakker sputtered, coughed, wiped the stuff from his eyes.

"Thank you for seeing me, Mr. Dakker."

Dakker fingered his bruised cheek. "Who are you?"

"I need to speak with you about your sons."

"Fuckin' brats. I am not gonna be responsible--"

"One of them died."

Dakker reached for one of the cigarettes. I slammed a cupped hand against his ear. "Don't touch that."

"Who the fuck--"

I curled the ends of my fingers, drove my knuckles into the soft part of Dakker's throat. His hands clutched at his damaged voice box, pulled at the flesh beneath his chin.

FROST

"You will speak only when it is necessary to answer my questions. Understand?

Dakker nodded.

"Your boy Paul is dead. Matt is still alive and he needs to be allowed to grow up. I represent some people who are willing to feed him, clothe him, see that he gets medical attention. They will get him into a good school and when the time comes they will see that he has the opportunity to go to college. He will be well cared for, happy and safe.

"I have a piece of paper in my pocket that you must sign for this to happen. Briefly, you agree relinquish all custody rights to the boy forever. You will never see him again. From what I can tell, seeing him wasn't much important to you, anyway.

"I'm going to reach into my pocket and get the legal document. I'm going to hand you a pen and you will sign it. When you've done that, I'll give you five thousand dollars in cash to forget we ever had this conversation. Agreed?"

Dakker's left eye pulled, blinked into a tight spasm. "What if I don't want to sign it?"

I picked up one of the lit Carltons. "Both of your sons are covered with scars, Dakker, the kind of scar that could only come from cigarette burns. If you don't sign this thing, I will personally hogtie you and see just how many holes I can burn into you with a full pack of Carltons, then I'll forge your signature and keep the five thousand for myself."

Dakker glared at me and his eyes began to dance. "Ten thousand."

I smiled, then crammed the burning cigarette into Dakker's cheek and held it there. He screamed in pain.

"Last chance," I said.

FROST

"Gimme the pen," he gasped.

Dakker signed the document. I tossed the cash on the table and stepped toward the door, then turned to face him. "One more thing, Dakker: I don't like you, and I'll be around. You don't want to hurt anybody, and I mean anybody, ever again. Understand?"

Dakker pushed out of his seat. "You got what you wanted, he said, rubbing his ruined cheek. "Get out."

I walked to the Mercury, fired it up and drove away. I'd just told a man his son was dead and the guy didn't even bother to ask me how it happened.

FROST

Chapter Thirty-Seven

I met Miles Wednesday morning on Broadway at an espresso stand next to Chase Bank. The brisk Autumn air gave everyone the opportunity to pull on sweaters they'd neglected since last winter and heavy boots. I wore Wranglers and black Justin cowboy boots with a black wool and silk blend turtleneck under a tan suede jacket. Miles wore a green and tan abstract monstrosity with crimson khakis and some kind of designer workboot.

Nobody noticed.

Miles ordered for us, a latte for him and since the coffee cart didn't have plain old fashioned drip coffee, an Americano for me. Armed with caffeine, we trekked back to Miles' apartment.

Serena spent the night with Matt and Donna, wouldn't be back until we called with the all clear.

Miles' computers never slept. I'd given him a list of recommended disbursement of Pear's money, included trust funds for Serena and Matt, and some padding for Miles and Donna Trent just in case of some kind of child-rearing emergency. I took a little padding, as well, but I left the amount to be padded up to Miles.

Miles researched legitimate charities devoted to child abuse and put them on his list, along with others dedicated to stopping hunger, providing medical care and housing, and animal rescue. I'd scanned his list, recognized a dozen or so, had never heard of some of the others, but the short end of it is that well above two-hundred and fifty worldwide charity organizations were going to examine next month's bank balance and find coffers filled well beyond their wildest expectations.

Every major new organization on Earth, whether internet, broadcast or print, would receive a video feed detailing the activities of Pear's chicken ranch clients accompanied by photographic proof. Law enforcement agencies would receive names and addresses of house locations with more than enough evidence to justify a warrant in those countries that require such things.

"You say this should all take about ninety seconds?"

"About that. You want to punch the send key?"

"I don't think so." I turned toward the voice. Camey balanced a Micro Uzi on her right hip as naturally as she might have clipped a cellphone to her pocket. "Lose the weapon, Micah, both of them. And you--" she waved the ugly little gun at Miles-- "slide away from that keyboard."

I tossed the Ruger onto the sofa. "Who was she?"

"A runaway. There are dozens. It was easy to find one that fit my general description."

"Why would Pear identify the body as you?"

"It would have been easier to claim the body as mine than to explain how an underage runaway wound up dead in his kitchen, especially considering his sponsorship of world-wide runaway shelters."

"That does explain why he didn't seem all that broken up over your untimely demise. You killed Wainwright."

"I did. Wainwright had approached me about getting rid of Pear. I thought about it, it made good sense, but you have to be careful with Pear. You never know what he's buried that might blow out of the ground and eat you when you don't expect it."

FROST

"Why include me in any of this?"

"You were a distraction, Micah, just that. Pear hates you for what you did to your father, blames you for everything that happened to the old man. I assumed that once you surfaced you'd probably kill each other. At the very least, Pear would be focused on you which would give me some time to finish hiding his assets."

"That was a mistake. Pear knew where to find me, long before you started your little game. I found his address book and my name and address was buried in the middle. If he'd wanted me, he'd have gotten me long ago. Why'd you order those three kids to kill me?"

"I thought you'd assume Pear had sent them."

"Why not just eliminate Pear?"

"Easier said than done, as you well know."

"And why Wainwright?"

"He had some stupid idea about a seventy-thirty split, his favor. I balked, and he offered to turn me over to Wiley and Robbie for target practice. It was simpler just to get rid of him. You and Pear walked in and found him, Wiley and Robbie cleaned up the mess. It worked out all around."

"So what now?"

"I'm set to transfer everything to a series of accounts in the Cayman Islands and then I'm going to vanish," she said, "but first I need those flashdrives."

"That's not going to happen."

"Yes, it is."

I dropped to the floor and rolled. Camey fired the Uzi and I felt a series of whistles above my head. I grabbed for the Ruger, rolled again, shoved the gun in front of me and fired, twice. One shot struck Camey in the shoulder, the other caught her in the thigh. She tumbled to the floor and the Uzi skittered out of her reach. I stood up, walked to where it fell and retrieved her weapon. Camey's eyes glowered in their sockets.

"Don't worry," I said. "You'll live."

"That has yet to be determined." Wiley and Robbie sauntered into the room from the kitchen.

"Miles, do you ever lock a door?"

"Frost, would you mind pointing that thing somewhere else?" Neither man had drawn their guns, so I lowered the Uzi and reholstered the Ruger. "Are you done with her?"

"I think the police may have a few questions. And the Feds."

"So does Stone. She can answer his first."

"You stupid imbeciles," Camey spat. "Grab--"

Wiley crossed the room in two steps and backhanded her, hard. "Miss Horne," he said, "you need to be quiet."

Camey nodded.

"You'd best get some compresses on those wounds, Wiley. Don't want her bleeding to death before you can get her back to Pear."

"We'll take care of it. We also need to get those flashdrives."

"That's going to be a problem, Wiley."

"No, it isn't," Miles said. He scooped up a handful of them and walked them to Wiley. "Just please go."

"Miles--"

"Forget it, Micah. I'm done."

I started to argue, thought better of it. "Okay," I said, finally.

FROST

Robbie draped Camey's left arm around his shoulder and wrapped his arm around her waist. I watched through the window as he mostly carried her to a black Cadillac Escalade and literally threw her into the back seat. Miles joined me at the window and we watched them climb into the vehicle.

"That went well," Miles said.

"You think?"

"I'm happy."

"They've got the goddamned flashdrives, Miles."

"Nothing on them. I wiped them when I downloaded the transfer codes to my laptop."

"Seriously?"

"I said I was done with them. You want to let's do this?"

Miles walked back to where his computer sat and punched two keys. "It's done, or at least it will be in about a minute and a half."

I watched the Escalade disappear around the corner. I never saw Wiley Sturgill or Robbie Long again.

I never saw Camey Horne again, either.

FROST

Chapter Thirty-Eight

On Thursday morning I took some of what had once been my brother's money and rented a loft near Pioneer Square. I paid a year's rent in advance and an additional five hundred dollar pet deposit. I'd be happier in an untainted space and Crickett would be happier with a larger open space to sleep in. I'd like to think she might occasionally run through the place, but in all the time she'd been with me I'd yet to see the dog run.

I stopped at a men's boutique near Capitol Hill and replaced the brown leather bomber jacket I'd lost when I drove the Santa Fe off the Harbor Island Bridge. I'd get around to replacing the lost ID in the next few days.

I arranged for my bank to cut a certified check to Enterprise Rent-a-Car for the Santa Fe. It was easier than answering a lot of questions from an Insurance Investigator, and besides I could afford it, now.

I also arranged for twenty-five hundred dollars to be paid to Charles Holmes. Once the money transferred, I donated the car to a charity that worked with wounded vets.

Donna Trent's story on Wainwright's disappearance made the front page of the Times and got picked up by a number of other news organizations. Speculation was that Wainwright had known the authorities were about to close in on him and he'd emptied his coffers and skipped the country.

Worldwide, news organizations scrambled to confirm the legitimacy of a series of photographs acquired anonymously, but with what appeared to be documented proof of authenticity. The photos displayed a number of prominent personalities in compromising positions with obviously underage partners. Wainwright figured prominently in the material and the news community quickly speculated that racketeering wasn't the only reason he'd decided to take a powder. Chances are, thanks to Wiley and Robbie, he was powder.

Steven Cook vanished, simply gone without a trace, at least as far as the public was concerned. The television station he'd hosted offered a twenty-five thousand dollar reward for information leading to his whereabouts. I thought about calling and suggesting they spend the money on something useful.

Sam Rollins called and informed me that SPD closed the Halleck house, arrested the staff and turned the kids over to Social Services. Police in San Francisco, Los Angeles and Las Vegas closed similar operations, as did authorities in Japan, Italy, France and Great Britain. The name Pearson Stone appeared on outstanding warrants in three states at this point, as well as on several Federal warrants.

I doubted they'd catch him.

***

I pulled the new rental car out of the parking lot and aimed for West Seattle, parked in front of my old house and climbed up the concrete stairs. My ex-landlord wanted some fourteen thousand dollars in damages and I'd transferred the amount when I transferred the money to Charles.

I wandered aimlessly through the place, decided what furniture I'd move and what I'd dispose of. I tunneled into the basement, gazed at Rapunzel and promised myself I'd redo the piece within the next week or so.

I heard a knock at the door. I climbed the stairs two at a time and hit the main floor just in time to see Chelsea step through the doorway. Crickett followed at her heels. The dog stumbled toward me and stretched out her left paw, and I slapped it lightly on the pads, *gave her five*, and she trotted to the couch and burrowed herself next to a padded arm. She slept almost immediately.

Chelsea wrapped her arms around me, kissed me deeply. I inhaled the scent of her hair, gently blew a lock from her eyes. I pulled her closer, held tightly, burrowed my face into the soft skin of her throat, and gently kissed the sweetness I found there.

The front door imploded into the living room. Pear cannonballed onto the hardwood floor, rolled to his feet and came up shooting. I shoved Chelsea into the hallway, hoped Crickett would find her way to the kitchen unharmed.

Pear barreled toward me, all five-foot-eight inches and three-hundred and fifty pounds of mostly muscle. He leapt and I ducked, but his fist caught the side of my face and slammed me into the brick fireplace. The room whirled and I fought to regain my balance.

Crickett leapt toward Pear's exposed throat. He absently backhanded the animal and she smashed against the far wall. I shoved an open hand into Pear's crotch, grasped as hard as I could and twisted, jerked him to the floor. Pear roared. I knocked the pistol from his grasp and punched him in the face, twice, and crammed a thumb into his left eye.

The room filled with a deep redness and suddenly Pear was on his back, bleeding from his ruined eye. Somehow the Ruger

FROST

found its way into my grasp and I pressed the barrel under Pear's chin, pushed the barrel into the softness beneath his chin and fired, emptied the revolver into my brother's skull. I heard dry fire, knew the gun held no more ammunition, and whipped the butt of the thing into Pear's cheek again and again and again until my arms could move no longer.

I stood, my clothes and my hands covered in my brother's blood.

Chelsea ran past me, bolted down the concrete stairs.

I picked up Crickett, ran my blood-smeared hands along her ribs and spine, and felt nothing out of place. She began to whimper, nuzzled my chest, and I knew the dog would be okay.

I heard Chelsea's car door slam, heard the engine roar to life, heard the screech as she skidded away from the curb. I dropped the empty Ruger onto the hardwood floor and carried Crickett toward the front door.

FROST

Micah Frost will return in

SECOND

SHOT